So This Is What Life Is

By Peter L. Campo

0

Table of Contents

INTRODUCTION

"So This Is What Life Is..." Is a fictional sci-fi adventure, as seen through the eyes of an ordinary guy named Henry. Who was tragically snatched from his average life and unwittingly confronted with the most complex challenges one could ever face. Was he destined to become the man he's always wanted to be.

As the story unfolds, it reveals elements of human behavior, which includes physical, philosophical, sociological, and spiritual components. The same ingredients that comprise our human existence. And, above all, it is a love story.

This author hopes, whether you agree or disagree with the story's fictional premise, you will sit back and enjoy the journey.

CHAPTER 1: Cecilia

To tell my story, which seemed to begin long ago… I remember one particular day; my adrenaline was surging through my veins as I stood on a mountaintop cliff. Some two thousand feet high, overlooking the vast valley sprawled out below. The foliage was beginning to turn yellow, brown, and orange. A fall breeze burnished my face as the cool sun beat down from the blue sky, interrupted only by widely scattered cumulus clouds. Why I was there was just a marker in the story of me painfully discovering myself.

A couple of years earlier, I met Cecilia and thought I'd finally found all that I was looking for. She was as close to perfection as one could get. I believed she was my salvation.

You see, since I was a boy, I had big dreams of doing things that had significants, as I believe all boys should aspire to. My chosen career was architecture. I studied and worked hard to become a architect. I envisioned someday of designing a community better than any ever built, and having a woman like Cecilia by my side fit into my grand scheme, which might've been a bit grandiose.

Right out of college, I landed my first job with the prominent architectural firm Andrews, Donnelly, and Seon. I felt I was on my way. Of course, I understood that I had to start at the bottom and work my way up from a mundane lineage.

Perhaps, mistakenly, I assumed that I would automatically move up the ladder and become the person I believed I was meant to be by working hard. Starting in the drafting department, I worked hard and became so good at what I was doing that I began to move up within three years.

After five years, I made history by becoming the youngest head of that department. However, at the same time, I realized that I was on the wrong ladder. Even though I was doing rather well financially and was an essential part of the firm's workings, I wasn't on track to design the community I'd dreamed of building.

My job was to see to it that the designs of others were transferred into workable blueprints. By being quite good at what I was doing, I inadvertently boxed myself into a corner, for the company wanted me to continue doing it. I stayed, which regrettably set a cap on the advancement of my dreams.

Back then, I was somewhat timid or perhaps naïve concerning the corporate world. Although I was well-liked and respected, I hadn't learned to navigate the corporate waters. I guess I was too much of a nice guy or perhaps even a wimp. I found it difficult to stand up for myself, promote my designs, and position myself as a front-runner.

The race to the top of the company was crowded with the best of the best. Consequently, to move up, I had to displace someone, which was an unpleasant thought. Being a nice guy, I found myself locked into a job that fell short of my dreams.

I became frustrated, for I believed I was capable of doing more important things. However, I can only fault myself for not taking the bold and uncertain path of stepping out and go on my own. Instead, I chose to submit to my bosses. As I now learned, I wasn't courageous or competitive enough to become independent and start a company of my own. For I feared the loss of the financial comfort and security my job had given me. My years of work had already achieved a steady salary, benefits, and a profitable investment program.

Therefore, since I lacked that kind of confidence in myself, I chose to compromise. I looked to other activities for the sparks I so longed to feel within my professional life.

To most, I appeared to be a placid, level-headed, regular

guy. However, inside, and as far back as I could remember, I envisioned creating extraordinary designs. Not for the sake of becoming important, for I'd already achieved it to some degree, but rather to accomplish something of substance in my own right. I was part of some significant projects in my job, but I played only a minimal role in the scheme of things.

After more than a decade on the job, and in my thirties, I felt my opportunities and creative juices had dried up. Perhaps out of cowardice, and to compensate for the lack of stimulation, I relied on my physical prowess more and more. I skied down Snowbird (akin to Squaw Valley), dived into deep waters, averaged 90-100 mph on the freeway (successfully dodging tickets). I even learned to fly a plane (although I couldn't afford to own one.) I substituted those types of highs instead of seeking the fulfillment of my dreams in my work. But not for one moment did I ever think there would be any consequences for this behavior.

So on that day, there I was, standing atop the escarpment looking down at the valley far below. Cecilia was patiently waiting down there for me to land. Invigorated by the breathtaking beauty, I was readying for my first solo flight. With the help of my instructor, I strapped on a hang-glider harness. As my heart pounded against my chest, I looked out over the vista below. My enthusiasm was tinged with fear.

I was just able to make out the flag flying atop the tower at the landing site, a speck in the far distance said to be miles away. It looked most formidable. Simultaneously, I was surprised and somewhat disappointed to see how many were lined up, waiting to take the same leap. My hope was by accomplishing this feat, I would achieve something exceptional. Yet, I found myself in line with others and saw the same feelings I was experiencing on their faces.

Nonetheless, the moment's reality was there, and the jump

certainly had an element of risk. I took deep breaths to calm myself and get the proper perspective. After the instructor helped me hook up to the rented Rogallo wing, my turn finally arrived.

He yelled, "Go! Go!" With a running start, I stepped off the cliff, leaping into space, which I must say took a measure of courage, for I never liked being up high. As I sailed out into the thermal updraft, lifting me up in my thrilling intoxication, I couldn't help but express screeches of joy.

As the wind coursed around me, I was like a giddy kid. I glided out and around for some distance, imagining I was a bird. At that moment, there was no place I rather have been, soaring high in the sky with nothing but air to keep me aloft.

Flying on my own for the first time was all I imagined it to be. It was close to having a mystical experience, almost as if I was flying among the gods. It gave me something I hadn't ever felt before, infused with unimagined empowerment. It made this effort worthwhile despite having to share it with many others.

All too soon, I had to bring my attention back to the moment. I turned my focus to the landing site—a huge bullseye target laid-out on the valley's floor. At first, it looked like such a small target. I maneuvered the wing towards it, controlling its direction as instructed.

As I sailed closer and closer, it became larger and larger, causing me to think perhaps it wasn't as big a challenge as I'd hoped. With others sailing around me and landing with ease, I felt as if I was just another small bird flying in the flock, not the eagle dominating the sky that I so wanted to be. Now, able to look back with clear vision, I see how shallow those types of endeavors were, although they seemed so important at the time.

However, at that moment, I hoped to land dead center on the bullseye. Awkwardly guiding the wing as I circled. I spotted Cecilia standing by the target, the size of an ant, waving her arms frantically, motivating me to do well. I recognized her by her new bright red coveralls, which had a broad yellow stripe running down her sides, an outfit she purchased, especially to share this occasion with me. I assumed she spotted me as well, for she insisted I wear an identical outfit.

With her free-flowing blonde hair, she looked as stylish and beautiful as ever. She was always concerned about how she looked, which I must admit I did appreciate. I always felt the need to impress her, although she never gave the impression she was seeking it. She was so beautiful; I feared if I didn't keep her interest in my physical proficiency, she would become bored with me. Not believing I had the kind of success that warranted her attention was another reason why I lavished gifts on her.

I approached the target at a fast rate, tilting the wing incrementally to slow down to a safe landing speed. I began to wonder if I would make it far enough to land where I'd hoped. Cecilia waved me in as my speed slowed. Luckily, I stalled two feet above the six-foot-wide black dot in the center of the target. I must confess I dropped down rather than landing, knowing it was more luck than skill.

Landing on my feet, I pranced around with a stylistic flair like a peacock, as if I'd done something remarkable, again just to impress her. Now, in hindsight, perhaps I looked more like a chicken.

Before I could unhook the wing, Cecilia, with a broad smile of relief, tightly embraced me as if we had been apart for an eternity. I understood how much she disapproved of me doing these types of stunts, which she considered not only dangerous but childish. Nevertheless, I perhaps blindly felt the need to impress her. I now see how I was not as considerate of her feelings as I should've been.

Quickly moving off the bullseye and unhooking the wing, I asked, "What did you think of that?"

"Henry, watching you up there, I was terrified."

"Oh, there's nothing to it. It was fun. You should try it."

"Oh no, you'll never get me up there. And don't even

try."

I laughed; although the truth was, if she were up there, I would've been concerned for her well-being.

I said, "Come on. It's time to celebrate. Let's go," not yet knowing what the future held in store.

CHAPTER 2 The Celebration

Cecilia and I arrived at Bernardo's, our favorite eatery, freshly showered and dressed in formal evening attire, for she liked the high life. My best friend Phil and his wife, Martha, were on their way to join us for a celebratory dinner.

Phil was a successful building contractor. His company, Modern Build, contracted a lot of work from the firm I worked for. Our relationship went back to grade school. I owed him a lot. For one thing, he helped me get my job.

Growing up together, we always encouraged and teased each other to do better, which I believed was the main ingredient for making both of us successful. Although I felt my success was only a financial one. Phil's triumph was well-rounded, being an established independent builder. I always felt my accomplishments paled in comparison, although I was as proud of his achievements as if they were my own.

Despite my lagging, he always encouraged me to follow my dreams, which I found not easy to do. However, his encouragement went beyond professional goals, for he was my biggest supporter and shared the sports challenges we both indulged in. His prompting only encouraged me more so to participate in what Cecilia considered to be hazardous activities.

As we waited, I could tell Cecilia was uneasy, for she knew Phil was the instigator who kept challenging me. Each time after conquering a new physical challenge, we celebrated with a dinner.

Cecilia never appreciated our friendship. Phil and I were buddies because we shared many of the same interests despite me always being a step behind. It was a fact lost on her.

However, I could see why her attitude towards him was so,

for he was somewhat of a braggart, and on top of it, he was always late.

Before they arrived, I said little about the flight and simply gave her solid gold earrings with dangling glider wings. She always showed appreciation for my gifts, regardless of what they represented.

They finally showed up, and not too soon, for I needed someone to unwind my pent-up pride in accomplishing today's flight. Although I knew that feeling would not last long, Phil would bring me back to reality with his joking. And I was right. As they joined our table, the subtle jabs began. "You made it, you fool. Sorry I missed it. I heard it was a smooth landing, however awkward. Trying to outdo me. Right?"

"Oh, it wasn't that great," I said, engaging in the game of playing it down.

Cecilia said, "I'm just glad he made it in one piece."

Martha said, "Oh, come on, dear. We're never going to tame the boys. Give it up."

To change the subject, I said, "Well… Let's order dinner. I'm famished."

The back and forth bantering continued while eating, as only close friends could do. However, knowing Phil so well, it was apparent he had something else on his mind. After the meal, he couldn't hold back any longer. First, he lit a cigar and then said, "Hey, wait till you hear this one. You're not going to believe it."

Martha added, "Cecilia, he's right. You're not going to believe it."

Cecilia said, with some tension, "I don't even want to hear it. But somehow, I know I will."

Undeterred, Phil continued, "Wait, you've really got to hear this."

Cecilia, sensing the direction he was headed, said, "No, Phil, we don't want to hear it."

I responded, hoping to pacify her, "Honey, it won't hurt just to listen." Shamefully, the truth was I wanted to hear it. And, regardless, we knew no one would be able to stop him. I put my hand on hers, attempting to soothe her. She gave me the look of it is not going to work this time and gently pulled her hand away.

As expected, Phil couldn't help but continue, "Henry, this is a new one, never tried before. Do you remember that guy Jonathan, the one from Alaska, at the club last week?"

"You mean that big burly ex-special forces guy or something?"

"Yes, that's the guy. Well, I had lunch with him yesterday, during which he told me of a jump north of the Arctic Circle, some five hundred miles out on the ice he hoped to make as soon as he could find others to go along."

Cecilia said, "I knew I didn't want to hear it."

I couldn't help but be intrigued, yet I had to mollify her. "Honey, it's only talk," I said, perhaps not being as truthful as I should've been, especially with myself.

Attempting to be helpful in his clumsy way, Phil said, "That's right, it's only talk." However, despite seeing her feelings towards him, he could not restrain himself and continued, "Imagine that, to jump hundreds of miles north of the Arctic Circle. Then driving back all that way on snowmobiles. Through uncharted territory to the edge of the ice pack to be picked up by a boat. Exciting, isn't it? Very few, if any, have done it in that way before."

Martha injected, "Boys must play."

With greater insensitivity, Phil said, "We could be on our way in just weeks, how about it?"

Indignant, Cecilia said, "We're getting married in a few months. Soon, he'll be a married man with responsibilities no longer able to act like a boy playing games."

Phil said, "Look at Martha and me... We're married."

"Yes, look at us," Martha said, with her dry cynicism as

she took a sip of her martini.

"He's not going to consider it. Right—Dear," Cecilia said—her eyes, now daggers, pointed right at me.

"Yes, honey." What else could I say under the circumstances? I never wanted to cause her any unhappiness, especially in public.

Because of our lifelong friendship, Phil felt he had a claim on me, and Cecilia resented it. I now realize it was unfair to her. I would give anything if I could now fix it.

After an uncomfortable pause, Martha said, "Let's order dessert, shall we?" Tactfully changing the subject as she made eye contact with Phil to indicate he should shut up.

Nothing more was said about his proposal, and the evening ended on a more pleasant note.

CHAPTER 3 The Agreement

Days later, while relaxing in our shared apartment, Cecilia and I were sipping wine while watching a movie on my seventy-two-inch TV. I'd been most fortunate in my work, along with still being a bachelor, it allowed me to enjoy more than a modest lifestyle.

Cecilia was the daughter of a high-level company associate who had some wealth. In the scheme of things, with my moderate success, I tried not to kid myself into believing it was my accomplishments alone that attracted such a smart and beautiful woman.

You see, I was always told I was good looking and was fortunate enough to have dated several beautiful women. However, I felt most fortunate to have Cecilia's love, for she was a ten in my book. Even so, as quickly as we became intimate, it still took me almost two years to have the courage to ask her to marry me, fearing she would say no and burst the bubble.

I could only imagine what she saw in me. Most likely, she liked me because I was a steady hard working guy who adored her. And I suppose my physical stature, tall with a well-built body, helped. I must admit we were a good looking couple.

However, I was just coasting at that point in my life, afraid to rock the boat. Never wanting our relationship to end, but thinking she might discover how weak I was under the facade, I successfully hid behind. At times, it felt as if I was walking on eggshells, always anticipating the next crack. Never fully able to live free and uninhibited. Looking back, I could only wonder why I accepted things being so, for I wasn't doing that badly. In fact, I had many good things going for me.

However, as we watched the action filled movie with its spectacular special effects, I couldn't help but drift off, fantasizing about Phil's proposal. I kept picturing myself going on that adventure. Of course, Phil couldn't stop talking about it.

Cecilia saw the forlorn look in my eyes and asked, "I hope you're not still considering that stupid trip. Are you?"

Conflicted, as the prospect of such a trip pulled me in one direction and my love for her in another, I meekly said, "Well... No..." again, I was not truthful.

Seeing my hesitancy, she said, "I know that look of yours. I always know what you're thinking."

I was never able to outright lie to her. I just avoided issues that might have caused me to do so. However, this time, it was different, and I courageously or perhaps foolishly said, "But honey, I must admit it's tempting, and in a way, I kind of wish I could go."

Disturbed, she lashed out, "I knew it! Look, just because I love you doesn't mean I want to marry a child."

"But honey, you know I've always done those things. It's not easy for me to change. Please give it a little time."

"Well... I do understand, but I don't want to marry a dead man."

"Wait a second. I'm not a dead man, and I'm not planning on dying anytime soon."

"Your ridiculous stunts frighten me. In just months, we'll be married, and I don't want to live a life filled with the fear of losing you."

"I'll be careful; I'll be just fine."

"Well, I'm not fine with living like that. I want things to be orderly and safe. Not knowing if you'll be coming back from one of your senseless larks, not knowing if I'll come home to find you injured, or receive word that you're dead—that's not the kind of future I envision for us. I want to have a family that's safe and peaceful, not fraught with meaningless dangers."

Unsure of what to say, I pulled her close and held her until she collapsed limp into my embrace. After a penetrating silence, I tentatively made a suggestion, "Honey, maybe we could make a deal?"

"A deal... What kind of deal...?" Again with daggers in her eyes.

"You know I want nothing more than to marry you and make you happy. And I know that you'll never be truly content if I continue to take on those challenges. So perhaps you'll allow me this one last shot?"

"You mean to accept you going on that dumb trip."

As if I was putting my head on a chopping block, I said, "Yes, I guess it's what I'm asking."

She looked at me, and I quickly interjected, "If you do, I'll promise it'll be the last time I'll do anything dangerous, ever again. I need this one last shot to get it out of my system... Maybe, if you can think of it as a bachelor's party, it'll be my final fling. I love you; please allow me this one last adventure."

Although I spoke with assurance, I now see that I wasn't truthful, not only with her but also with myself. I couldn't see my fault at the time, for I was captivated by the allure of the trip.

"You rascal, you know how to smooth talk me. I love you too. It seems I've been waiting to marry you forever, and I don't want to lose you."

"You're not going to lose me. I promise, just this one last time. I promise."

"Oh... You charmer. If it's not the last time, you'll be in big trouble. Remember, if you don't keep that promise, I'll kill you myself. First, you must promise me you'll be alive to marry me."

"I promise, I promise." She smiled and gently whacked me, and we made love.

CHAPTER 4 The Adventure Starts

With the trip settled and my vacation time approved, Phil and I dove into the preparations. First, we met with Jonathan, our expedition leader, to commit ourselves to the trip. Since we knew almost nothing about the Arctic, we followed his directions and shopped for the proper clothing and equipment he thought necessary, much of which was done online.

Phil insisted we buy the best. Being the wealthy one, he also paid all of Jonathan's expenses in taking us, in return for his expertise and leadership. Being a savvy businessman, Phil understood Jonathan's intent when he first met with him was to acquire the financial backing for the trip. However, Phil didn't care, taken in by the allure of the adventure. Alas, I had to pay my own way, and it cost me plenty. If I were smart, I should've bought a sports car instead.

When the big day finally arrived, Cecilia, Martha, Phil, and I drove to the airport. Each of us was in a solemn mood, for none of us looked forward to the separation. We had our last breakfast together in one of the better airport restaurants.

At the boarding gate, Cecilia squeezed me so tightly I could almost feel her heart trembling. Even though she had come to terms with me going, it just about broke my heart to leave her. However, I felt compelled to do this, figuring I'd be back in no time ready to enter a lifelong commitment with her. Never considering any other result.

My hope was this last bold endeavor would get that compulsion for adventure out of my system. As we parted, I was full of optimism. Perhaps I was too childish to understand what I was doing—as Cecilia kept telling me.

Having our gear shipped ahead, we checked in with our carry-on bags. Once in the air, I let my feelings of excitement lose as I envisioned what was ahead. Fascinated with the view below, I watched every mile of the landscape as Phil snoozed.

Jonathan had gone ahead and was waiting in Fairbanks.

After catching up with him, there was enough time to do some sightseeing. Neither Phil nor I had been this far north. Still, in a state of disbelief that this was indeed happening, we hired a tour guide and enjoyed seeing the sights in Fairbanks.

Not long after dinner, we turned in, having to catch an extra-early flight to the top of the continent the next morning.

When I got up in the morning, I was filled with nervous anticipation, which kept me from getting much sleep. We consumed an ample breakfast and a ton of coffee. After this, we took off in a single-engine, propeller-driven, DeHavilland Beaver plane. It was a noisy and bumpy ride, although comfortably warm. We landed on a small airstrip outside Barrow and were driven in an all-terrain vehicle to nearby buildings. Distinguishing them from the surrounding landscape was difficult, for they looked more like snow-covered mounds than buildings.

Once fed and settled in the warm and comfortable housing, Jonathan took us to a meeting room of sorts. He stood like a military commander, which was natural for a Special Forces type guy. With pointer in hand, he tapped a spot on the wall map. "Gentlemen, tomorrow we'll leave without delay from this point here, and travel along this route, ending up at this point, which is approximately five-hundred miles north out on the ice, where we will jump. I'm sorry about the rush, but, up here, there's always the danger of the weather closing in on us. Right now, it looks clear and good to go."

I asked, "Where are the snowmobiles and supplies?"

"As you know, all of our equipment was shipped ahead. Don't be concerned, for everything will be on the plane waiting for us. There are three snowmobiles and three trailers packed with more than a sufficient supply of fuel, food, and everything needed to make it back. When we jump from the plane, the flight crew will eject everything out at the right moment to land as close to us as possible.

"Everything, including us, is equipped with sensors, so we'll be able to locate the supplies and each other after landing. As I'm sure you understand, if we lose anything critical, the trip will be over. In case of a real problem, a rescue team will locate us with a GPS and bring us back. That's unless the weather closes in, causing us to wait it out.

"Gentlemen, we must leave at four hundred hours. Since this time of year, the skies remain lit around the clock. To better acclimatize yourself, relax, and tonight get sufficient sleep.

In the morning, dressed in our pricey cold-weather outfits, we were ready to go. Beforehand, out of fear of delaying the trip, Phil decided not to tell Jonathan we'd never parachuted from a plane before. However, we did study how to do it on the internet and, of course, I went along with it. With those first-jump jitters, we carefully strapped on our parachutes, making sure Jonathan checked us out. We headed out into the bone-chilling air and boarded an old cargo plane that was waiting with its propeller-driven engines running.

Strapped into rather crude seats, we took off into the clear skies. Flying at five thousand feet and only kept warm by our cold-weather outfits, hoods, gloves as we wore oxygen masks. It wasn't long before the uncovered parts of our faces felt frozen. I would've paid extra for a heated flight.

It seemed to take forever, traveling over the almost-frozen water and then the hundreds of miles more, over the endless snow-covered ice. I began to feel the cold penetrating my clothing and wondered if this would be as much fun as I'd hoped—for I never liked the cold. Preferring to be sitting in the hot sun, on a beach with a chilled drink in hand.

Finally, and not a second too soon, we reached and circled the jump area. The terrain looked rough, not like we envisioned it should be. The flight crew lowered the ramp at the tail of the plane, allowing the bitter wind in. As we hooked up our pull cords, the flight crew quickly pushed the equipment out.

Jonathan boldly jumped first, followed by an eager Phil. When I looked out, I must admit I felt a little queasy, for it looked quite inhospitable. However, a crew member gave me a nudge, knowing it wasn't wise to wait for a second longer. I forced myself to jump.

Parachutes filled the sky, looking as if a small army had invaded. As I sailed down, the endless snow-covered vista left me in awe of its forbidding magnificence. The parachutes were made with an assortment of colored material, which contrasted with the white snow, making it easy to spot them. It took about twenty chutes to get the equipment and us down safely, for each piece needed two or three of them.

With this new jumping experience, I was beginning to enjoy the ride, for it put another challenge under my belt. I could see why people got their thrills from skydiving.

With some confidence, I guided my chute, much like the hang glider. The three of us landed reasonably close to each other and the equipment.

Jonathan landed the closest to a snowmobile, even though it was still a hike for him. He radioed us to wait for him to pick us up. When he did, he drove us to our individual snowmobiles and trailers.

We were surprised at how the terrain was riddled with ice spikes instead of being smooth and flat as expected. The spikes were similar to stalagmites, ranging in size from a few inches to about three feet tall, scattered throughout the landscape. Was this a bad omen for what was ahead? Luckily we weren't impaled upon landing. Even Jonathan showed concern, not knowing what to make of the spikes. Despite those obstacles, its alien beauty was breathtaking.

When everything was hooked up and ready, we headed back on the long trek home, which I now must confess was a pointless trip. All that was to be accomplished was nothing more than having bragging rights.

CHAPTER 5 Disaster

Traveling at a moderate speed, it was quite a wonder to see the gleaming white snow having faint hues of gray, green, blue, and black as the full light spectrum reflected off it. We wore tinted goggles to protect our eyes from snow blindness.

Moving in zigzag patterns to avoid colliding with the larger of the dangerous pointed obstacles, it wasn't only strenuous on our muscles but also our minds, for it required our full concentration to navigate the landscape. In time, we drove out of the spiked area and stopped for lunch and a much-needed rest. While heating the food on a tiny propane stove, Phil said, "Isn't it beautiful, the air is so pure?"

Jonathan said, "It's one of the last untouched places on earth. At times, I wish I could stay out here."

I could only say, "I might agree if it wasn't so cold," even though I was building up a sweat under my insulated clothing. I tried not to say anything negative as not to be thought of as a wimp, for I found Jonathan was not only exceptionally macho but a little strange. However, given his background, he deserved our respect.

Both he and Phil were in better physical shape than I was. Despite my being naturally athletic, I spend most of my time sitting at a drawing board in recent years.

With a chuckle, Phil said, "Well, let's eat before the food freezes solid." As we gulped down the hot soothing coffee and devoured the food, Phil asked Jonathan what was ahead.

He painted a picture of how unpredictable and volatile this place could be. How storms and upheavals had their way as the ice shifted, often in an unexpected instant.

I must admit, Phil and I had no idea of those dangers beforehand. I guess we only saw the glory in our boy-like fantasies. We listened to him as if we were kids listening to the elders around the campfire, being fearful yet intrigued and enthused by the challenges.

Unfortunately, experiencing unusual things wasn't something I often found in my job. I lacked the opportunity to create work of my own that was both inspiring and innovative. Although my company had accomplished some impressive projects, my part was small. I foolishly believed this trip would be my chance to prove my worth. Yet, I didn't know to whom or what end.

I'd felt as if something was missing in my life that I had to find for some time. Regardless, due to my promise to Cecilia, I understood this might be my last opportunity to act out the missing pieces I thought I was looking for. On the other hand, I wondered if it was going to eliminate those unfulfilled cravings of mine. I hoped to return home content to live a life in safety and peace with Cecilia, for my wish was to make her happy.

Turning my focus back to the adventure at-hand, we mounted our machines and took off. We frequently stopped to rest so as not to exhaust ourselves. In time, and only indicated by our watches, the day ended. With daylight remaining around the clock, the light hardly diminished. Even though it had only been a day since our arrival, the never-ending daylight seemed to throw off my metabolism.

We set up a tent under clear and calm skies, ate dinner, and then packed into our sleeping bags. The sleeping bags were made of a new high-tech paper-thin material that kept our body's heat in. Quickly falling asleep, we slept like babies, comfortable and warm to dream of what tomorrow would bring.

Jonathan's alarm watch woke us early; our twenty-four-hour watches were the only way to tell whether it was day or night. However, while we were asleep, an overcast set in. With no sign of the sun, not much light penetrated the mist. It looked more like late evening than morning. We warmed with a hot breakfast, packed our tent, and once again were on our way.

It was dark enough to turn on our headlights, which cast long eerie shadows against the white topography. It felt as if we were aliens trekking across a forbidden land. Fearing worse weather, we moved as fast as Jonathan thought safe in the hope of breaking out into the clear.

Despite the dangers, Phil and I couldn't help but challenge each other. We raced in short competitive spurts of speed, each trying to outdo the other. We were enjoying ourselves, like kids in a playground, not fully grasping possible dangers. Jonathan kept radioing us to slow down and to stay in line with him, driving at a safe speed.

As time passed, instead of breaking out into the clear, the fog thickened. We tightened up as not to lose sight of one another. It went reasonably well for a time, although we couldn't help but be concerned.

Suddenly! And without warning, the ground began to shake and rumble violently. It felt like an earthquake as a massive shifting in the ice took place. The surface rolled and rippled as cracks appeared around us. I was terrified, afraid to stop, not knowing what to do. Instead of cool heads prevailing, we sped up in the hope of driving out of this trouble spot. Even Jonathan was rattled.

The wind sped up as the snow swirled up and around, engulfing us until we lost sight of one another. Panicked, I continued to move ahead, which was the biggest mistake I ever made. I hoped I was still between the two of them, doing my best to avoid the dangers. Accomplishing it with momentary success, it was like riding a rollercoaster with obstacles.

Then, with a thunderous cracking sound, a deep crevasse split-wide-open in line with my path. Having no time to react, to my horror, I drove right into it.

Hugging my snowmobile while falling, I knew for sure I was a dead man. In that instant flashing by in my mind's eye, I saw how my foolishness led to this devastating consequence. As I fell, I deeply regretted those difficult athletic challenges of mine in those milliseconds, which was now causing my demise. Stupidly, I chose not to take the best advice given—especially from Cecilia—that to indulge in risky escapades was a death wish. Having given that idea little or no credibility, preferring to make excuses. I looked in all of the wrong places for the missing sparks I imagined I needed.

As I continued to fall to my death, an unlikely occurrence took place as the walls closed back in, inadvertently catching the snowmobile with me on it in mid-air, avoiding a hard landing. My unconscious body was compacted in the ice.

(Meanwhile, Phil and Jonathan had lost sight of each other on the surface and pulled up despite the dangers. Shortly, just as suddenly as it began, the shaking subsided, the crevasse was now closed, and the thick mist slowly began to dissipate.

The two of them were able to locate each other using the instruments. However, they couldn't determine my coordinates. When able to see clearly, they desperately drove around searching for me. Their GPS devices picked up a weak signal, but as they zeroed in on it, it appeared to be coming from well below the surface. At first, they hoped the readings were a malfunction.

Desperate, they called in a Mayday. As they collected their thoughts, and despair set in. In time, exhausted and at a loss, they reluctantly gave up the search fearing my fate was a disaster. They just sat there, stunned, waiting for help to arrive.

Overwhelmed, Phil was hardly able to speak and moaned, "Poor, poor Henry. What am I going to tell Cecilia? What have I done...? She asked me to keep him safe. How can I ever face her with this? She'll never forgive me. I'll never forgive myself, poor Henry."

"Yes, it's a tragedy. Henry seemed to be a good fellow."

"He was my best friend, and I talked him into doing this. How will I ever be able to explain this to her?" Phil said as he bowed his head and cried uncontrollably.

"I'm sorry," Jonathan could say little else.

After an unbearable wait, two helicopters appeared in the now-clear sky. In the upheaval, they both lost their trailers, and with no hope left, one of the helicopters hoisted them up, abandoning their snowmobiles. They disappeared into the endless sky, leaving the other helicopter to continue the search. It circled the spot for miles around until their fuel was too low to continue. Only then they left the desolate area.

The search continued for days using GPS and visual sightings, covering the entire area. Since the GPS signal was so weak, the rescue team landed and walked the area where the signal was the strongest. However, since they ascertained it was coming from deep below the surface, they deemed I couldn't have survived that long being buried in the ice. Therefore, after trying their best and by no means able to dig and recover my body, I was left to be forever entombed in the ice.

The winds gusted, covering up the snowmobiles, turning it back into the seemingly untouched terrain as if nothing had occurred.

(The authorities officially ruled Henry's disappearance as a fatal accident.)

CHAPTER 6 The Awakening

Time passed, the winds blew, and the snow fell across the tundra, layer upon layer, as the ice shifted in the Earth's endless rotation. Continuing the half-year seasons of 24 hour light days followed by a half year of 24 hour dark days.

Due to the natural changing of weather patterns, in time, the Earth warmed. Mountains of ice at the poles melted, causing massive icebergs, some cities' size, to break away and float towards the equator exposing the Arctic Ocean's waters. In the wake of the melting, it caused water levels to rise worldwide as the world flooded, creating new coastline configurations leaving much of the land underwater.

The last remnants of the melting ice lodged on the newer rugged coasts to the south to meet their end. One day, along one of the coastlines, several children, girls and boys alike, all dressed in identical gold coveralls, ran towards the shoreline as others watched from the cliffs above in the distance.

What drew their attention was something sticking out of the side of a bus-sized chunk of ice beached on the rocks.

Reaching it, a discussion ensued.

One asked, "What's that?"

"It looks like The Machine," another responded.

"What's it doing here?" the third asked.

"Is it really part of The Machine?"

"I don't think so. Its color is not the same."

"What else could it be?"

"I don't know."

"Could it be broken?"

"The Machine never breaks."

"Then, it's not part of The Machine."

"Look! There's something else in there." They rubbed the surface of the crystal-clear ice, pressing their noses against it trying to see what was sitting only inches from the surface.

Another asked, "What could it be?".

As they examined it, another said, "Look at that!" and as they did, it frightened them. Screeching in horror, the youngsters all ran back to those watching from the cliffs above.

Shortly, a large number of gold-colored ball-like flying objects appeared. None bigger than softballs. They swooped in and around the piece of ice like a swarm of bees, beeping incessantly as if examining it with sensors that penetrated its surface. Then, as one, they all flew off.

Moments later, two car-size wingless airborne disks arrived. Without hesitation, they began cutting into the ice with laser-type beams. One cut out the machine as another cut out the coffin-sized block containing the object that frightened the children. With those two pieces firmly in their clutches, they carried them off, leaving the children silently watching from the cliffs.

The flying disks approached a vast shining golden city on a hill surrounded by high mountains on one side and the ocean on the other. Midway up in the taller of the only two skyscrapers, an outside door slid open, allowing the hovering craft to enter.

Once inside, the items were carefully unloaded by mechanical means. A smaller disk with tentacles picked up the coffin-sized block and carried it deeper into the complex. Delivering it to a gold-colored room, for everything was that color, and placed it on a platform.

With no person visible, a light beam coming from the ceiling scanned the block. And a stream of warm air blew gently on it as vacuum tubes efficiently sucked in the melting ice and dirt.

As this process continued, an audience gathered to watch from above. All dressed in the same gold outfits as the children wore. They sat behind tilted plate glass windows—much like those in hospital operating rooms. Eerily observing, looking more like statues than real people.

Seated among them, a noble-looking young woman asked, "Is it a person?"

A tall, slender white-haired man said, "Sara, The Machine indicates it is."

"Oh, how interesting," she said, mesmerized as she watched.

It wasn't long before the ice was gone, and the object was dry. What remained was a lifeless purple prune-like human figure wearing clothing with gloves covering its hands and a hood on its face. Apparently, that image is what frightened the children.

Apparatuses emerged from behind panels in the walls, which contained probes with grips, and gently stripped away the figure's clothing, as beeping sounds filled the space. When done, what remained was a barely recognizable freeze-dried shriveled-up nude body of a man.

Other strange-looking apparatus emerged from separate compartments in the walls. Among them, a vibrating device gently massaged the stiff and lifeless body, as others administered different odd-looking procedures. The onlookers watched in morbid silence.

The woman called Sara asked, "Who is he?"

The man pressed a touchpad on the wall and listened. Then said, "The Machine does not recognize him as one of ours, and he has been frozen for some time. Sadly, he is in such bad shape he might not rejuvenate. I am afraid we will have to wait to see if he will come back to life and if he does, I imagine it will take time."

"I hope he will survive."

"Sara, The Machine will hydrate and give him nutrition along with the necessary treatments. Beyond that, you know there is nothing we can do to help. In this situation, we must trust The Machine."

"Father, sometimes, I wish I could do more."

"Now Sara, you know better than that. We gave away the right to interfere a long time ago."

"I understand. Meanwhile, when able, could I hold his hand?"

"Perhaps, if and when permissible, but you must be patient. Your caring soul is a gift never to be lost." He left as she continued her vigil.

She sat behind the glass for hours at a time, day after day, as others came and went. After non-stop treatments, the stranger slowly put on some bulk, much like a balloon taking in air. A device was placed over his mouth and nose, forcing air in and out, attempting to breathe life back into him.

In time, his dead skin began to shed as new skin magically grew under the old. Now apparently, having life, he was starting to look more like a human being.

Improving, he began to breathe on his own, ever so weak with the attached devices' assistance. He remained unconscious. A levitating piece of equipment moved him to a more intimate room onto a soft bed. People were now free to enter, although only to watch silently.

Sara was now able to hold his hand. Due to his emaciated condition, most would find it an unpleasant task, yet she was unperturbed by it. As the days passed, the number of people watching diminished until only a few were in and out for short periods. She was the only diehard.

Her vigilance was unwavering, holding his hand for extended periods, only leaving to eat and sleep. Still unconscious, his dry skin continued to shed, as moist baby-like skin replaced it.

As the days passed into weeks, the equipment continued to administer its seemingly miraculous functions.

Then, one day, she felt his hand twitch in hers. The Machine beeped. She called out with alarm, "Father!"

Although he wasn't in the room, he soon appeared and asked, as if he had heard her, "Sara?"

She said, "He moved ever so slightly, and The Machine signaled. What does it mean?"

Father, as she called him, went over to the touchpad on the wall. He tapped one of the different colored spots, and a series of sounds responded. After listening intently, he explained, "There's no need to worry. It's the first sign of his recovery."

"Is he going to get better?"

"Things are looking promising. There's a chance he will."

"What can I do to help him?"

"All you can do is exactly what you've been doing. The Machine is keeping him in a suspended state until he's strong enough to wake. If The Machine cannot help, you know there is nothing we can do."

"Yes. I understand… Thank you Father."

They exchanged smiles, and he left.

Turning her attention back to the stranger with the patience of a saint. Although frustrated, there was nothing more she could do other than holding his hand. Yet, that simple act seemed to transfer her determined spirit to him, for in his condition, it was extraordinary he would ever come back to life.

As each day passed, he improved, although looking not quite real. Eventually, all his dead skin shed and vacuumed away, making it easier to look at him.

Then one day, his comatose body began to stir and jerk uncontrollably as The Machine beeped loudly. Alarmed, she grasped his hand more tightly as the echoing sounds drew a curious crowd.

Father entered and tapped on the touchpad; he listened intently,
then said, "Do not fear, it is a good thing. His life has been restored. Sara, be patient. I believe he will soon wake."

Expelling her breath, she said, "Oh, that's wonderful to hear! Waiting has been most difficult."

He smiled. "Yes, but you're so good at it. Keep it up, and you'll reap the fruits of your compassion." He left, and with a subtle smile of contentment, she turned back to her task.

Before long, his recovery was phenomenal. However, he was still gaunt and in an unconscious state. Since Father said he would wake soon, she could hardly wait as she sat by his bed, holding his hand, not wanting to miss that moment.

However, it took a while longer before it would happen. Meanwhile, she only left his side to eat and sleep only when assured he wouldn't wake in her absence.

That moment finally arrived as my eyes popped open. Confused and with a sense of wonder, I looked around and mumbled something incoherent.

"You're safe now," Sara said, trying to calm me as she squeezed my hand. "Everything is going to be all right."

I again attempted to express myself but was unable to articulate it. With my speech gobbled and unrecognizable, my frustration grew.

Sara called out, "Father! Father!" he came quickly, and she pleaded, "Please help!"

He tapped on the pad and again listened. Then spoke to me, "Your vocal cords are swollen and need to shrink before you will be able to speak clearly."

Panicked, I again attempted to say something but was unsuccessful.

She said, "Please relax. You'll be able to talk soon." Still agitated, I tried to sit up but was too weak. A visible beam of light touched my head from the ceiling, which instantly put me to sleep.

Father instructed, "While he is sleeping, you must rest. Meanwhile, The Machine will heal his voice."

"Father, how can I rest with his life in the balance?"

"Sara, you are a wonder. You know The Machine will take care of him. Still, since you persist, your sisters will not leave your side to make sure you have sufficient food and rest."

"Sorry Father. I don't understand my feelings. All I know is I must look after him."

"Child, it's always best to follow your feelings, for you are one of the dwindling Special Ones."

She said, "Thank you Father." He left, and she turned her attention back to me. Several young women entered, who he had called her sisters, closing in around the bed in silence—never saying a word.

Determined not to leave my side, she even slept there—confident her sisters would wake her if I awoke.

(She longed to find out who this man was and where he came from. Having spent her entire life within the boundaries of the shining golden city, she could only imagine what lies beyond those limits. Fantasizing about him gave her a feeling she'd never experienced before, one of excitement, opening new vistas in her imagination. All she could do was hold his hand and plead in her heart he would soon wake, only to dream of what that moment would be like.)

CHAPTER 7 Recovery

The next day, my eyes opened suddenly for the second time. The girl greeted me with exhilaration, "Hello, my name is Sara, and these are my sisters."

I looked at them intensely, not knowing what to think as they closed in around my bed. It felt as if it were a dream. Now, able to speak, I asked, "Where am I?"

She said, "You're in a rest-room."

"A restroom? What am I doing here?" Confused, not understanding what she meant by a restroom.

"You had an accident and are being renewed."

"An accident! What kind of accident?"

Don't you remember what happened to you?"

"No, I don't remember an accident. What accident?"

Father entered and said, "We are pleased to see you are finally awake. Welcome to Ohganiea. I am called Father. What is your name?"

Still bewildered… I had to think for a moment before answering. Then I said, "Henry Bender." I didn't know what to make of these people, for it all seemed so surreal.

"Father, he does not remember what happened to him."

"I see." He tapped the pad and listened to its communication, which sounded like someone speaking extremely fast, beyond recognition. He didn't comment.

I asked, "What is Ohganiea?"

"It is our island land," she answered.

"Your island land? I've never heard of it."

Father calmly said, "You've had a traumatic experience which took your life. You may not remember what happened right now, but, in time, I believe your memory will return."

"Took my life? How did I get here? Am I dead?"
She said, "You were rescued from the ice."
"What ice? And where's Cecilia?"
"Who is Cecilia?" she asked.
"Where's Phil?"
Father asked, "What's the last thing you remember?"
I racked my brain, trying to sort out this shocking information. Recalling, I said, "I remember being in Bernardo's, with Cecilia, Phil, and Martha." Unnerved, I asked again, "Where are they? Have they been called?"
Father said, "For now, you must rest."
I saw a beam of light touch my head, and I was asleep.
"What's wrong with him? Why must he sleep?" she asked.
"Now Sara, you know The Machine does not like to sense distress. All this information might be too much for him to absorb all at once. We must inform him slowly as his memory returns. However, at the same time, we must find out who he is and where he comes from, hopefully before The Machine does. Today he will sleep. Please have something to eat and get some rest. Remember, you will need your strength when he awakes."
"Yes Father, I will," she said, as she and her sisters obediently followed him out of the room.

The next day, I awoke more alert. The girl said, "Hello Henry Bender," her pitch was melodic and welcoming, which lifted my spirits even under these dire circumstances. Still confused, I looked at her young angelic face, and for a moment, I thought I might be dead and in heaven with a beautiful guardian angel. I then remembered her name and said, "Hello, Sara."
"Henry Bender, how are you feeling?"
"I'm not sure, but I'm awful thirsty."

"Yes, you've not had real food or drink for some time."
She tapped the touchpad, and almost instantly, a tray appeared out
of the wall containing a square biscuit and a container.

Seeing my bewildered look, "She said, "Take it, it's
feeding you. It will not harm you." She uncapped the container,
and I guzzled down the strange but pleasant-tasting drink. Which
immediately soothed my parched throat. After examining the
unappetizing square biscuit, I cautiously bit into it. I was amazed
at how good it tasted with its unfamiliar mixture of flavors. I
devoured it and found it quickly satisfied my hunger.

I said, "Boy, that was good."

Henry Bender, "Do you feel better now?"

"I do. Where's Cecilia?"

"Cecilia? I'm sorry, I do not know. I will see if she can
be found."

"I must see her. When can I leave this place?"

"Where do you come from?"

"Why New Haven of course!"

"I have never heard of New Haven."

"How can anyone not hear of New Haven? Where am I?"

"Ohganiea."

"I've never heard of it. Where is it?"

"It is our island land."

"Island land? Where's it near?"

"It is not near any other place."

Her simple answers only confused me. I'd never seen a
room like this, where everything was gold-colored, and things
suddenly appear out of the walls. All the women in the room
wore the same gold outfits. Were they nurses? They were
attractive as I imagined nurses to be, only they had blank childlike expressions on their faces as they gazed at me, never saying a
word.

Sara was different; she smiled and was talkative. To wake
up in a place, I'd never heard of, with these strange people around

me was really creepy.

She asked, "Henry Bender, do you remember how you got here?"

"The last thing I remember was eating in Bernardo's."

"What is Bernardo's?"

"It's a restaurant where we were having dinner."

"And you do not remember being frozen in the ice?"

"Frozen in the ice? What ice? Why I hate the cold. What do you mean?"

"You were found in the ice by the shore."

"That's impossible. Do you have a phone; I must call Cecilia and Phil."

A bit perplexed, she said, "Be patient. We are looking for them. Now you must relax and get some rest."

"I must call them," I insisted. As I struggled to get up, pulling at the things attached to me, I saw that beam of light touch my head, and I was asleep.

Father entered, she said to him, "He was upset and asked for something called a phone. The Machine then put him to sleep. Why must it do so?"

"Sara, you know it does not like agitation. Please remain calm."

"He was only trying to figure out where he was and what happened to him. He only remembers being in a place he called a restaurant named Bernardo's and asked for a phone."

"That is interesting. But remember, something traumatic happened. We must take care in how we bring him back to life. If not, it might make him worse."

"He keeps asking if we called this Cecilia and Phil. What does he mean?"

"Sara, I am not sure, but I believe it has something to do with a phone. I will see if I can find out. Remember, remain calm."

"Yes Father."

"Good. Now have something to eat and get some sleep, for he will not wake until tomorrow." She obeyed, leaving with her silent sisters.

When I awoke the next day, it took a moment to take in the surroundings, only to realize I was still in this strange place. I was lying on a bed with just a sheet covering my naked body.

That angelic-looking girl was sitting by my side, holding my hand. I managed to say, "Hello, Sara."

"Hello Henry Bender. How do you feel today?"

"I'm not sure. How long have I been like this?"

"Thirty-one days."

"You mean, I've been like this for a month!"

"Yes. However, it couldn't be determined how long you were frozen before you were found."

"Frozen? What do you mean? I don't understand."

"The Machine told Father; in time, you will regain your memory. Please be patient, it will soon come back."

"The Machine?"

"Yes. It is helping you. It brought you back to life."

"Brought me back to life? Where's Cecilia? Where's Phil?" I was utterly befuddled and needed them more than ever.

"We do not know. If you can remember what happened and where you come from, we might be able to find them."

"Where I come from? I told you I'm from Connecticut. From New Haven, Connecticut."

"I am sorry. I am not familiar with New Haven, Connecticut."

"Where are we?"

"Ohganiea."

"Ohganiea! Where is it again?"

"As I said, it is our island land."

"Your island land? Where am I really?" All this was incomprehensible. Was this a dream I couldn't wake up from?

Seeing my confusion, she repeated, "You are in Ohganiea."

"I've never heard of it! Have you called Cecilia?" I was beginning to lose my cool and sat up.

She looked as confused as I was, calling out, "Father!" Then said, "Please, Henry Bender try to relax. Father will be here in a moment," as she squeezed my hand.

"Where's Cecilia?" I asked again.

"Who is Cecilia?"

"She's my fiancée."

"What is a fiancée?"

"We're going to be married soon."

"Married?"

"Yes! Where is she?"

"I am sorry I do not know."

"You must call her!" I said as I tried to get out of bed. I saw the beam touch my head, and I was asleep.

Father entered, and she said, "The Machine put him to sleep again. Must it always do that?"

He tapped the pad and listened, then said, "He was upset, and you know how The Machine does not like distress."

"He was only trying to express himself. How are we to learn about him? And this Cecilia he is calling for if he is always put to sleep?"

"Sara, The Machine has no record of him or Cecilia. We must trust The Machine knows these things."

"Does it really know?"

"Now, Sara, keep calm. You know better than that."

After a thoughtful pause, she said, "I am calm, and I am sorry Father. I just want to know who he is and for him to be well."

"Sara, you must understand he might not only be from another place but possibly from another time. By asking for a phone, I found out it was a communication device that is now a long-forgotten relic. When he learns this, he might become internally confused, and you know how The Machine reacts to that type of behavior. It is best to bring him back slowly from his bad experience."

"Yes, Father, I understand."

"Good, now please take this time to relax, eat and sleep, for he will not wake again until tomorrow. You will be pleased to hear that The Machine also indicated he will be ready to get up and perhaps walk by tomorrow. You will need your strength to show him around our city and help him adjust to our ways."

Delighted in hearing that, she said, "Yes Father, I will be ready tomorrow." They all left together, leaving me alone.

CHAPTER 8 Discovering The City

When I opened my eyes the next morning, Sara was sitting by my side, holding my hand. With a number of those women, the ones she called her sisters, surrounding us. Could they be nuns? However, I didn't think so, for their outfits were a far cry from the traditional black and white habits.

I asked, "Tell me again, what happened to me?" I was beginning to accept the notion that something horrendous took place—yet I hadn't a clue what it was.

She said, "All I can tell you is you were found frozen at the shore, and The Machine brought you here to restore your life."

"Restore my life?"

"Yes. Your life was suspended in death, frozen in the ice."

"How could I've been frozen?"

"The Machine does not know. It does not know who you are or where you come from, which is most unusual, for it knows all the people."

"I'm Henry Bender from New Haven, Connecticut."

"Henry Bender, we cannot find your name as being one of us, and I have never heard of New Haven."

"Ask Cecilia. She knows who I am."

"It does not know of Cecilia either."

Bewildered, I could only ask, "Where am I again?"

"Ohganiea."

"I've never heard of this place either."

"Would you like to see it?"

"Why... Yes, I guess I would."

She went to the wall and tapped different spots on the pad

and to my amazement, all the apparatus attached to me automatically withdrew, disappearing into those compartments in the walls.

Unexpectedly, the bed rose to a vertical position, allowing me to stand nude as the sheet dropped away. I tried to cover up the best I could but could hardly move. With all those women staring right at me, it was quite embarrassing.

Then, as if by magic, a gold outfit, the same worn by everyone else, emerged from another compartment. An invisible force manipulated my every move to my absolute astonishment, quickly slipping the outfit on my pitifully thin body. From another hidden compartment, a crooked staff floated over to me. I took hold of it and supported myself as I stepped away from the bed, fully decked out in my brand new attire.

As they watched me being dressed, I assumed that they must have seen every part of me in all the time I'd been here. Believing they were on the medical staff gave me some solace, which allowed me to relaxed a bit, although it felt strange not wearing underwear.

A portion of the outside wall slid open, the women parted, and a thin disk flew in. It was just big enough to hold a seat wide enough for two. Sara sat on it and motioned for me to sit with her. I was still weak, and with the help of the six-foot crooked staff, much like I saw Moses carrying in the movies, I braced myself and walked over to join her.

Looking out, I was amazed to see we were tens of stories above the ground overlooking a sprawling golden city. I was enthralled, for it was unbelievable. Again I could only wonder what this place was? Thus far, I'd gotten so few answers.

Then, to my further shock, the disk sailed out, leaving the building behind. It propelled us high above the city. As I nervously looked around, I grasped the seat for fear of falling off. However, I felt an invisible force holding me in place as if I was strapped in. When sure I wasn't going to fall, I couldn't help but screech in sheer joy as we maneuvered above and around the city at super speed. I was overwhelmed, for this jaunt was right up there with the greatest of any amusement park rides I'd ever taken. When I calmed down a little, Sara began describing her city. Remarkably, the force field not only kept us in place but also kept the wind out of our faces as if encapsulated.

Looking down, thinking I should have seen automobiles in the thoroughfares far below. But all I saw were flying disks sailing around us. This incredible city was surreal with an unnatural atmosphere. Its gleaming gold color was highly polished, looking like it was made of solid gold. It was like a cartoon fairytale city one sees in the movies. Again I questioned, was I in a dream?

However, its ambiance was cold and hard. There was little noise as disks of all sizes flew above and below us. Some were built to carry only one individual, while others were made to carry various numbers up to a full busload. Since no one seemed to be steering them as they traveled at tremendous speeds, I concluded they had an advanced sensory system to keep them from ramming into one another. No human could react that fast. They were only about two inches thick, too thin to contain any engine I knew of.

I could only conclude this was not my world. What was this place? The entire shining city seemed crafted out of one solid piece of what looked like gold to my further wonder. Viewing it with my architect's eye, it was unsettling not seeing any true horizontal or vertical lines in its construction. The buildings had rounded soft edges and corners and drooped here and there, giving the impression they were about to fall over. It was like nothing I'd ever seen.

There stood only two distinctive gold skyscrapers tens of stories high among the numerous edifices, piercing the clouds, which dwarfed all other structures not built any higher than a few stories, yet built in the same precarious manner. However, since none of the buildings had fallen, I had to assume they were sound.

Naturally, since the disks maneuvered at all levels, there was no need for roadways. Instead, the spaces between the buildings appeared to be promenades filled with people wandering about. I was speechless as I peered in all directions, not knowing what to think or even ask. I could see Sara was delighting in my expressions as I marveled.

We flew to just beyond the populated area into the countryside. To a place, she called The Wilderness. Circling it, I saw it wasn't a wilderness at all. It was picturesque, carefully designed, and laid out in pleasant, colorful patterns filled with flowers, manicured grass, and pruned trees.

Upon landing, the force holding us in place automatically shut-off. With the staff's help, I was able to slowly shuffle along, still being quite stiff and wobbly. Holding my arm, she led me along one of the golden cobblestone paths that meandered through the area.

Being an architect, I couldn't help but be in awe of the symmetry of it all. The colorful birds and the fauna and flora were like none I'd ever seen. People crowded the area.

As we walked, she explained, "If it were not for the Wilderness, people would not have a place to retreat to. Here, a person can escape to the calming sounds of nature for extended periods giving them peace."

I said, "Yes, it is much the same as parks serve in New Haven."

She told me how she spent a lot of time out here. I could understand how this space gave her a calm manner. To my dismay, she further explained that The Machine constructed everything and maintained the meadows, streams, walkways, and even cut the grass.

I could only wonder what she meant by the singular expression of calling it all The Machine. But I hesitated in asking too many questions, for as yet, I'd no idea who these people were. Therefore, I listened to her as she told me how she liked walking, sitting, and running here. Relating how often she wondered what was beyond her island land

I was charmed by her, but as extraordinary as she was when I looked at the blank faces of the others around us, I had the impression something was lacking—notably when she concluded with a, "But."

"But what?" I asked.

"Well, I've always wished I could travel beyond Ohganiea."

"Why haven't you?"

"It is said there's nothing left out there."

I dared to say, "When I look into the eyes of the others around us, I only see blank expressions, not like yours. You have a glow they don't have."

"I do? I am not sure. Since I was a child, I have been told I was one of the Special Ones."

"Special Ones? What does that mean?"

"I do not know."

"Haven't you asked? Aren't you curious? I know I would've been."

"As a child, I used to ask but was always told to put my full trust in The Machine. You see, questioning has always been discouraged. Therefore, I eventually gave up asking. It was easier that way."

"Hmm. That's interesting. Does this Machine control you?"

"No! It takes care of us."

I paused, not wanting to say anything to offend or upset her. These people were strangers, and I still felt uneasy in this unbelievable situation. I thought it would be best to keep my negative thoughts to myself.

She thoughtfully said, "I was always told I was Special, and when I saw you, I sensed that you were Special too. Other than Father, there's no one else I feel that way about. Yet I don't know how to explain my feelings."

"Oh… No one ever considered me to be Special. And with all that's happening to me, I feel completely helpless."

"Henry Bender, I would like to know where you come from."

"As I told you, I come from New Haven, Connecticut."

"Where is that?"

"It's on the Northeast coast."

"We are on our island land, and I have never heard of New Haven, Connecticut, or anyplace else."

Her strange answers only confused me more so. I suddenly grew weak in my knees and faltered in my step. She ordered, "You are not yet strong enough to stay out for long. Let us go back."

Amazingly, the disk, which had been hovering close behind, caught up with us as if it heard her. Boarding it, I realized how exhausted I was and was glad to sit.

I said, "I just wish I could find out what happened to me."

Grasping my hand, she said, "Father will be able to help. Relax for now." We sped back to the city with unbelievable speed. It only took seconds. However, instead of taking me back to that bland hospital-like room, she took me to my new quarters, which she called my unit.

High up, we entered through an outside sliding door into my unit in the shorter of the only two skyscrapers. The inside had the same gold colored walls with only a few sketched thin horizontal lines of different colors. I found it uninspiring. Looking around, I could understand why the people spent as much time as possible in the Wilderness.

She said, "I will arrange a meeting with Father. Until then, you need to rest. But first, sit with me at the table. It is time to eat."

Famished, I said, "Yes, I am hungry."

With a mischievous smile, she tapped a touchpad built into the tabletop. A compartment on the table opened and produced two small trays, each contained a biscuit and a container filled with a blue liquid. As hungry as I was, I was disappointed it wasn't steak and potatoes, and impulsively said, "Is that it?"

"Is it not enough?"

That was rude of me. I then recalled how the biscuit I ate earlier satisfied my hunger and said, so as not to offend, "I'm sorry. It'll do just fine."

She tapped another spot on the pad, and a six-inch-wide ring rose up from another compartment. I looked at it curiously. She passed her hands through the ring, saying, "You must purify your hands."

"Ah," I said. Fascinated, I passed my hands through it and felt a tingling sensation. Again, she chuckled at my wonderment.

"Are things different in New Haven?"

"Oh yes. Entirely different." I took a bite of the biscuit, and again it was full of incredible flavors I'd never tasted before. The drink was also pleasantly different. "Boy, that was good." Placing the empty trays back in the open compartment—it closed and disappeared.

"Henry Bender, please tell me about New Haven, Connecticut."

As I described it, she was enthralled. Her eyes lit up, revealing a beautiful innocence, which overwhelmed me. I'd never experienced anyone like her and thought again this might be heaven, and she was an angel.

She asked, "Will you be going back to New Haven, Connecticut?"

"I must. Cecilia must be going crazy by now, not knowing what happened to me."

Her eyes cast down as she expressed an "Oh…"

I couldn't help but react to her overt expression of disappointment. Even though I didn't know her at all, I didn't like seeing her like that and quickly said, "You'd like it there."

Her eyes lit up again as she said, "Oh, yes, I would like to see it."

"I'll take you there."

"Would you?"

"Why not!" I exclaimed. Just then, a wave of weakness hit me, and I had to brace myself.

She ordered, "You must rest until you are strong enough to go back to New Haven."

"Yes, I will. I guess I've done too much on my first day out."

"I will leave you to sleep."

"No, don't go." She smiled and led me to the bed. As I laid down, a light beam from the ceiling touched my head, and I was asleep.

CHAPTER 9 Suffering The Great Tragedy

The next morning I awoke suddenly. I sat up to see a biscuit and drink sitting in an open compartment on the table. There was an open sliding panel in the wall, which contained a sizeable rectangular ring big enough to walk through.

I figured Sara set this up for me. It wasn't hard to figure out that it was a waterless shower. However, I didn't know whether to undress or not. Being modest and feeling vulnerable, I dared to pass through it fully clothed. A tingling sensation reverberated throughout my body, and to my surprise, I found it not only cleaned and refreshed my body but my outfit as well. Even more impressive, my teeth felt clean, better than ever before, or so it seemed. I wondered if all these inventions were healthy. In my day, for an architect, not having to design a plumbing system would've been revolutionary.

In this world, everything was tucked away in slots or compartments out of sight. It was weird, for there was nothing personal lying around in the open as if no one lived here. Wondering where Sara was, I felt very much alone as I ate breakfast.

However, I did like the room service, even if it was only a machine. This morning's biscuit and drink had a distinctively different flavor from the others. I assumed it was from the breakfast menu. But where was Sara?

To my relief, she soon appeared. Saying, "Good morning Henry Bender, how do you feel today?"

I didn't ask where she'd been, for I guessed if she wanted me to know, she would've told me. I answered, "Why, I feel completely rested. The Machine put me to sleep again, didn't it?"

"Yes. I believe it will until you are well."

"It's incredible. We have nothing like that where I come from. It's a lot better than sleeping pills."

"What are sleeping pills?"

"Oh, it's a medicine we swallow when we can't sleep."

"Swallow medicine! That is interesting. You must tell me more. However, Father is waiting. I hope he will be able to help us."

"Yes, us! Well then, shall we go?" I rather liked her referring to us, as us.

The wall opened, and on a waiting disk, we flew off.

Again, the ride was so thrilling I couldn't help but react with delight. She joined me as we both shrieked with excitement as we headed to the top of the taller of the only two skyscrapers.

It took only seconds to soar up to its top. An entrance panel slid open on the outside of the building, where we flew in and disembarked. I assumed there were no interior hallways, stairways, or entrances. The disks entered only from the outside directly into each unit.

Inside, this time we entered a large room. It was void of furniture, where a dozen or so men and women sat on the floor on cushions around Father. I couldn't help but notice how each person exhibited a different degree of alertness. In fact, one even seemed to have nodded off. The most alert was Father, who said, "Come and join us."

I felt apprehensive in this austere space, whose color was also gold, although there were three-foot white and black checkerboard squares on the floor. I wished I knew what to expect?

Provided with cushions, we sat among them. It felt as if I was called to the principal's office, although Father's tone was soft and non-threatening.

He said, "Sara told us you come from New Haven,

Connecticut?"

"Yes, sir, I do."

"Have you been able to remember how you got here?"

"No, sir. The last thing I remember was being in Bernardo's with Cecilia, Phil, and Martha."

"Who are those people?"

"Cecilia is my fiancée, and Phil is my best friend."

"I'm not familiar with the word fiancée."

"It means we are planning to get married," I said, as I was beginning to see how strange and different these people were. Again wondering where in the world I could be?

"I am sorry that I do not understand some of your words. I see this is going to be more complicated than I anticipated."

I asked, "What's complicated?"

"You see, when you were found frozen by the shore, it was evident you came from another place."

"Yes, I'm from New Haven, Connecticut."

"That is what is confusing. The Machine indicated that New Haven was once a city in the United States of America."

"That's right. Wait! What do you mean was once?

"I am afraid, as the oceans rose, New Haven was covered over and is now underwater."

"How can that be! I was just there a month ago. What's going on?"

Sara gently took my hand and said, "Henry Bender, I'm sorry, The Machine always tells the truth."

Father said, "Henry, remember, you were frozen for some time."

"How long was I frozen?"

"We do not know. What date do you last, remember?"

"Well, it was… Yes, it was September."

He asked, "September of what year?"

"Why, of course, it was September Two-Thousand-Fifteen." I immediately saw expressions of shock on their faces. Even the one who had dozed off perked up.

I asked, "What's wrong!"

With sadness, Sara said, "Henry Bender, I'm so sorry."

"Why?" I asked, sensing what they were going to tell me was not going to be good.

Father calmly said, "You see, our year is Four-Thousand-Forty-Seven."

"What! How can that be?" Suddenly, I saw what happened to me in a flash of my mind's eye. I was on a snowmobile sailing into that crevasse in the ice. Then the horror struck me. If this is a couple of thousand years in the future, Cecilia and Phil would no longer be alive. The thought of never seeing them again overwhelmed me. I broke down, uncontrollably pounding my fist on the floor in despair, crying.

Sara reached for my hand, but I had to wave her off, for I couldn't share the sheer pain of my foolishness. I collapsed on the cushion, consumed by a feeling of great sorrow. As others slipped away, Sara remained, quietly comforting me with her presence.

I had no idea how long I stayed like that, but I sensed it was quite a while. When I again became fully conscious of where I was and able to control my emotions, I sat up to see Sara and no one else. Not knowing what to do, I could only say, "I'm sorry."

"Henry Bender, there is no need to be sorry. It has been a terrible shock for you…"

After a moment of silence, she asked, "Would you like something to eat?"

"No, thank you." Despite feeling her compassion, I said, "Please, I would like to be alone for a while."

She said, "I will take you back to your unit."

Once there, I again asked if I could be by myself. When alone, grief overtook me as I cried out, "Oh Cecilia, oh Cecilia—what have I done to you? What have I done?" I collapsed on the bed, facing the loss of my love and life, along with realizing how much pain I must have caused her. I suffered from that great sorrow and bewilderment until the light beam touched my head, and I was asleep.

When I awoke the next day, Sara was silently sitting by me. She didn't press me to say or do anything, which suited me just fine. It took a few days before I felt emotionally strong enough to venture out.

We flew to the Wilderness and walked without saying a word. I realized I had to pull myself together, for there was nothing I could do to change things back to the way they were. I could say little about the past that was not full of pain. Consequently, for days, I barely spoke.

She insisted we take walks in the Wilderness to hasten my recovery. I even attempted not to lean on the support staff. With her help, I was beginning to feel stronger and able to focus on my survival, for I understood if I didn't, I would just die from the sheer pain of the loss.

To divert my thoughts, I turned my attention, the best I could, to this new mysterious city, which was now going to be my home. A place designed far beyond anything an architect of my day could've imagined. Constructed of one continuous piece of an unknown material, which at first I thought was gold. However, the floors were warm and felt like wood under my feet. The walls were soft to the touch, not metallic at all. I knew of no material like it.

Sara tried her best to explain how The Machine did all the labor without any input from people. It was incredible, which caused me to want to learn more. However, when I asked why the people lacked expression, she couldn't give a clear answer.

This intrigued me, for it was a challenge, which gave me the incentive to further experience this world.

Still, I couldn't avoid lapsing back into my grief. I tried to explain to Sara what I was feeling, "I loved Cecilia and intended to spend the rest of my life with her, but, because of my stupidity, I lost all I cared for and probably crushed her. I'm so ashamed of myself."

"Henry Bender, it was so long ago."

"To me, it was just like yesterday."

"Ah, yes, I understand. I never experienced the loss of someone I cared for. It must be most difficult?"

"It is. You're lucky. Although, sadly, that day comes to all of us."

She said, "Father is the oldest person in Ohganiea."

"Everyone calls him Father; is he your real Father?"

"Why yes, he is."

I asked, "What about your mother?"

"All older women are our mothers."

I was struck by that strange concept and jokingly said, "That's a pretty big family?" for I couldn't believe what she said.

"Family? I do not know that word. What does it mean?"

"You must have a word for the family?"

"I do not know of family. Tell me what it means?"

"I can't imagine you don't know what family means."

She looked at me with that innocent smile of hers and shook her head no.

I tried to explain it as simply as I could. "It's when a man and woman marry and live together, and, while being together, they produce children. That's what a family is." I felt a little silly in saying it that way, but I was never good at explaining such things.

"What is meant by being together?"

Speaking to her of such matters was like talking to a child, although, in other ways, she seemed more mature than I. Yet, she radiated an innocence I'd never seen in an adult before. As diplomatically as I could, I said, "It's when a man and woman in love come together and have intercourse." Now, that was awkward.

To my surprise, she said, "Will you show me!"

Oh boy, that shook me. However, I was still too weak to physically react to it, but under different circumstances, if I had the opportunity, I would've immediately done so. She was attractive, and when she held my hand, I felt her warmth, like being with Cecilia. Yet, I oddly sensed if I took advantage of the situation, I'd be violating something pure and precious. A feeling new to me.

I quickly said, "It's been a hard day, and I feel a little weak. Let's talk about family another time?"

"Yes, of course, you need to rest."

She left me to my thoughts, most of which were images of Cecilia and Phil. It broke my spirit to know I'd never see them again. When alone, I could only cry out, "What have I done?"

Fortunately, The Machine, as always, put me to sleep before my sorrows could overwhelm and kill me, for the pain was that great. If it weren't for Sara being here, I'm not sure I would want to go on living.

CHAPTER 10 Assimilation

The next morning I awoke late, exhausted, and feeling weak. The first thing I saw was Sara's sweet smile, and as usual, it perked me up.

She said, "Henry Bender, are you hungry?"

Of course I was. I got up, passed through the ring, and joined her for breakfast as if we had spent an intimate night together—although we had not.

Incredibly, for the first time since I've been here, I had the urge to use the toilet. I guess having been entirely dehydrated, my body absorbed all I had consumed thus far. Since I hadn't seen a toilet, with little choice, I asked where one would be?

She replied, "What is a toilet?"

Her not understanding my verbal explanation, I crudely pointed to my private parts and used hand motions to indicate I had to relieve myself. It was embarrassing.

She understood and tapped another spot on the pad. A wall panel slid open, which revealed a small space with a platform and a cushioned seat with a hole in it. I guess some things never change. I looked it over and asked where the toilet paper was.

"What is toilet paper?"

I said, "Well… When done, how does one clean themselves?"

With a smile, she said, "By the cleanser, of course. When you're finished, tap the red spot on the wall."

Stepping into the compartment, I was relieved when the panel slid closed, giving me the privacy I needed.

While using the facility, I speculated that they probably didn't use the toilet often with their restricted diet. When finished, I tapped the red spot and felt a vibrating sensation in my private parts. When ready, I only had to touch the door for it to open. I was relieved to now know how to deal with that necessity.

Sara asked, "Henry Bender, what would you like to do today?"

"I don't know. Wait... I think I would like to see how your city works up close."

"Then that is what we will do. What is meant by works up close?"

I chuckled and said, "Come on, I'll explain as we go."

On a disk, we scooted down to one of the promenades between the buildings. We disembarked and walked among numerous people, who appeared to be wandering about aimlessly. Even those traveling on disks at ground level seemed to lack a sense of purpose as they coasted along. It was depressing to be among them.

Scattered about were park benches filled with men and women. Again, what struck me was their blank expressions, as if drugged. The contrast was stark compared to Sara's lively spirit.

I asked, "What do these people do?"

"What do you mean, do?"

"I mean, like where do they work?"

"Work? Another word I do not know."

"I mean, how do they earn a living?"

"Oh, Henry Bender, you have so many expressions I do not know."

"How does one buy their food and pay their rent?"

"The Machine supplies our food. What is meant by buy, and pay rent?"

I asked, "How does one earn money?"

"Money? Henry Bender, I do not know how to answer your questions."

Could it be? They eliminated poverty and now share everything with no need to work for what they get?

I asked, "Then tell me who runs things?"

"Henry Bender, again, I do not know what you are asking."

"Sara. Who tells you what to do? Who teaches you? Who makes the rules?"

"The Machine does."

Finding that scenario hard to accept, I said, "Sara, you're going to have to show and explain that to me."

"Yes, I will show you more."

Stepping onto a disk, we headed to one of the several sprawling buildings. Inside its portal, there was an enormous open space crowded with hundreds of people lying on their backs on what looked like comfortable bean bags or more like inflatable chaises. Each person wore an odd-looking helmet-like contraption on their heads covering their eyes.

I was familiar with interactive computer games and assumed that's what they were. To be sure, I asked, "What are they doing?"

"They are living."

Fascinated, I asked, "Living?"

She said, "You can see for yourself," as she directed me to take a seat. Upon sitting, one of those helmet-like contraptions automatically levitated down onto my head, covering my eyes.

She ordered, "Lay back and look into it."

I made myself comfortable and looked into it. I saw an assortment of three-dimensional shapes. It felt as if I was in the picture, although only as a spectator floating in space. It was something I'd never experienced. But of course, this made sense, it was now two thousand years in the future, and nothing would not be possible.

At first, I assumed it was a form of entertainment. Although, I only saw different ambiguous shapes. Confused, I lifted the apparatus and asked what I was seeing. Seeing my expression, and before I could say anything, she grabbed my hand and said, "Henry Bender, come with me."

A disk took us up to the second floor through a large opening in the ceiling. The floor was only about six inches thick in a room that was at least one hundred feet square with no visible means of the structural support needed for such an incredibly thin floor. In my day, it was impossible to build such a span without a more substantial structure. Indeed, it would've collapsed.

On this floor, people were also reclining. Only this time, they were listening to what sounded like discordant music that filled the room. They seemed entranced but had the same blank look on their faces. After standing there for a couple of minutes and listening to the strange sound, I began to feel ill and asked Sara if we could leave. Although I couldn't understand why the hypnotic tones and atmosphere affected me, giving me an intense feeling of discomfort.

Not knowing what to think, she led the way out. It didn't matter which disk one boarded, for they were interchangeable in crowded areas. The nearest empty one just floated up to us.

Once outside, we moved at such a speed within seconds, we were in the Wilderness.

Silently, we walked along for a time. She then asked, "Henry Bender, what is troubling you?"

"I'm not sure. It's just…what was going on back there was disturbing."

"Why?"

"Because those people were like zombies, and I was beginning to feel like one of them."

"Zombies! What are zombies?"

"I'm sorry. You see, in my world, zombies are fictional characters who are grotesque and frightening, although they could be comical as well. They're called the living dead."

"The living dead! Why that sounds frightening."

"I'm sorry about calling your people zombies. What I mean is they're lifeless, without expression, nothing like you.

"Those are the old people. I am still young and called Special."

"I'm glad you are. Anyway, they don't look that old."

"How should old people look?"

"Well, I would expect older people to have wrinkles and be stooped over."

"That sounds strange. What is meant by wrinkles and stooped over? Is that what old people in your world were like?"

"I'm afraid so. Wrinkles are when one's skin shrivels up and stooped over means that one is no longer able to stand erect."

"How awful! Although, sometimes, I wish I wasn't so young and different."

"Why? You're perfect!"

"No, I am treated as if I was not normal. Being protected and looked after all the time. There are few I can express myself to. Henry Bender, I know you are Special too."

"Believe me, I'm not special."

"Oh, yes, you are. The Machine said so."

"The Machine told you that?"

"Why no, but Father interprets its language for he helped build it a long time ago. He said it does not recognize you, which makes you Special."

"That's interesting. I must ask him about that?"

"Yes, it will help you to better understand us."

Feeling weak, I asked, "How about going back to my place and having something to eat."

On the way, I asked, "How do the disks know where to go?"

"If one thinks it, it just knows."

"That's fantastic. Do you mean it can read your mind?"

"I don't know. It is just the way it has always been."

Seeing she had no concept of how extraordinary it was, I changed the subject as not to confuse her in asking technical questions.

During lunch, still trying to figure out this place, I again asked, "Where does the work take place?"

"Henry Bender, what is meant by work?"

"You don't have to call me by my full name."

"What should I call you?"

"Just Henry is good enough. What's your full name?"

"Why my full name is Sara."

"Don't you have a last name?"

"You mean a second name like yours? Why no, should I?"

"How does one tell which Sara you are?"

Amused, she said, "Each of us is known without mistake."

"How does anyone know which family they belong to?"

"Family? As I said, I do not know what the word family means. You said it has something to do with getting together?"

I saw where this was headed and wasn't ready to go there. I changed the subject, "How about showing me where things are done?"

"What do you mean?"

"As I said, I'd like to see where people work."

"If I knew what work meant, I would show you."

"I know you said The Machine runs things, but someone must tell The Machine what to do, right?"

"As I explained, The Machine tells us what to do."

"Okay… Then show me where that's done?"

"Why, it's done wherever it is."

"You showed me people sitting around doing nothing or watching something like interactive TV. Yet, they're not involved in making decisions or running things. Is that all they do?"

"Yes, it is all we do."

"Who built the city? Who grows the food?"

"Of course, The Machine does all that."

"You mean it does all the work and thinking?"

"Yes, it does everything."

"Where are the doctors who took care of me?"

"The Machine took care of you."

"Are you saying it's the brains behind everything?"

"Yes, I guess that is what I am saying?"

"That's remarkable. Does anyone know more than The Machine?"

"Father is the wisest among us. He has been here since before The Machine took over. And then, of course, there are the Special Ones. Oh my… But that is not to be known."

"Not to be known? What do you mean?"

"I should not have mentioned it."

"Why?" I asked.

She changed the subject and ordered, "Please, Henry Bender, let us finish eating."

Seeing her reluctance, I didn't pursue it, not wanting to upset her. Although she appeared to be stable, I wasn't willing to test those limits, for she exhibited moments of fragility as well.

However, my curiosity was percolating, for I was beginning to feel an enthusiasm for this new adventure. I felt there was something not only strange but also mysterious going on here, perhaps even sinister. I had to find out what it was without stirring things up, for I feared if I caused too much of a ruckus, there might be consequences to pay. Much the same as might happen in my world.

In my world, I couldn't imagine anything more interesting. In a way, I felt this adventure was what I always craved. With renewed hope, I said, "I want to know more about your world. Please show me?"

Obviously pleased with me asking her, she said, "Henry Bender, where would you like to start?"

"Show me again what people do. And, by the way, simply call me Henry."

"Oh, Henry Bender, I like the sound of your full name."

"Oh… Okay, call me what you will. Now let's go and see your world."

"Yes Henry Bender," we mounted a disk and took off.

Our next stop was in another large building that contained an auditorium where again, I heard music, only with a difference. Instead of an audience entertained by performers on a stage, the audience were the performers. Hundreds of people filled the room. All sat on cushions and held a rectangular object on their laps, not much larger than a carton of cigarettes, and, by tapping their fingers on its smooth surface, they produced the orchestrational sounds.

Despite all the instruments looking exactly alike, they created many different sounds. Together, it was a loud symphonic sound and beat, unlike anything I've ever heard. It wasn't only mesmerizing but also angelic as I imagined what that might sound like. It captivated me, although the performer's expressionless faces again struck me as being most odd.

After listening for a time, Sara motioned for us to move on. On the way to the next place, she asked, "Henry Bender, what did you think of that?"

"It was impressive. However, everyone there had the same look. Doesn't anyone enjoy themselves?"

"Enjoy? I do not understand."

"Sara, you are so different than any of them. They lack your zest. Why are you so different?"

"As I keep telling you, they are the elderly, and I am still young."

"Where I come from, old people still had life and expressed themselves."

"I do not know how to answer you. We will have to ask Father about that."

"Okay, then we'll ask Father… What's next?"

"Would you like to meet the children?"

"Yes, I would. I've been wondering where they were?"

CHAPTER 11 Meeting The Children

I hadn't yet fully grasped what Sara meant by the old and the young. So far, the oldest-looking person I'd seen seemed to be still in their prime. Although most of everyone's expressions lacked life. Curiously, I hadn't seen any children. I assumed they were at school or perhaps living somewhere else with or without their parents.

Flying beyond the city into the hills, we approached a large area surrounded by a four-foot-high wall where the ocean was visible in the distance. It contained no tall structures, instead only twenty-five-foot-circular gold-colored mounds, which appeared to be constructed of the same material as the city was.

We landed in an open space within the walls to find energetic youngsters, about fifty or so of all ages and noticeably, no adults. With a roar of excitement, they rushed to meet us— crowding around our disk. They ranged in age from their teens to as young as toddlers. As we stepped off the disk, they became eerily silent. Their stares penetrated me.

A boy who looked on the brink of manhood asked, "Sara, who is this?"

"This is Henry Bender. He is from another place."

An "Ah!" rippled through the group. A small child said, "There's no other place."

An older child asked, "What other place?"

"It's a long story. For now, Henry Bender would like to see how you live."

The boy asked, "Are you the one we found in the ice at the shore?"

"Yes, he is," Sara said and then introduced the boy, "This is Roger. He is almost too curious to come out into the city."

He said, "From what I've been told, I guess I am. Anyway, we will show you how we live."

I asked, "Roger, isn't being curious a good thing?"

He answered, "Due to The Machine, I am told not to be that way."

"Roger, you know better than that," Sara instructed. Their little exchange seemed odd to me, and I wondered who and why he would be kept out of the city. For some reason, I didn't pursue it. Instead, I followed their lead as they showed me their living conditions.

Thin sleeping mats lined the floors of most of the mounds, which were void of furniture or any of the comforts of home, including personal items. There were about a dozen mats per mound, with no privacy afforded. Each child wore the same gold coveralls. I learned they only owned one outfit each, which they wore all the time. They relied on the cleansing rings located in one separate mound to keep their bodies and outfits clean.

Naturally, their clothing had to be replaced as they grew. When I asked about that, I was taken to a mound filled with identical outfits of all sizes. Sara explained as each child grew, they would choose the next larger size from the collection of previously worn coveralls from generations past. I thought how economical they were. These children grew up with hand-me-downs, nothing like the consumerism that plagued my times. A bare-bones existence, in utter contrast to my world. No sixty-inch TVs. No well-designed, comfortable places to relax in. No electronic gadgets or games to occupy their time. Just living with the most basic means and a minimum of food and shelter.

Upon finishing the tour, a wailing sound went off, as loud as an air-raid siren. Sara said, "Henry Bender, it's time for the children to eat."

"Please don't go! Eat with us," Roger pleaded.

I asked Sara, "Could we?" My curiosity was not yet satisfied, and I was hungry too.

"Henry Bender, we can try," she said.

Roger said, "Good. Follow us."

The dispensing machine was in a separate small mound, which contained two ports, with a hand-cleaning ring sitting by each one. The children lined up at each station. I was impressed by their aptitude for cleanliness. Although it was The Machine that did all the work.

I was taken back a bit by the well-ordered waiting line protocol; I hadn't done that since my grammar school days. However, I also stood in line, hoping to discover more about these children's conditions.

With a biscuit and drink in hand, Roger led us to a spot on the grass. My preference was to sit at a table for a meal. But there were none, nor chairs for that matter. It seemed they were kept much like domesticated animals.

How insensitive of these people, giving their children no more than the most basic essentials. Plus, little or no interactions with adults. Although I realized how spoiled I had become in my former life, yet all this seemed beyond the pale.

As we ate, the children clustered around, eager to hear every word. Roger questioned me, "Where do you come from?"

Sara injected, "Henry Bender comes from New Haven, Connecticut."

"Where is that?"

"It was in another time," I said, still finding it hard to accept or explain.

"What! You mean you travel through time?"

"No, it's not that way at all."

"When you found Henry Bender, he had been frozen in the ice for a long time; The Machine restored him," Sara added.

"Yes, and I want to thank all of you for finding me and saving my life. If the ice had melted before you found me, I certainly would have died."

Wow! Tell us more?" Roger exclaimed as the wide-eyed children were enthralled. With Sara's help, I explained what occurred, at least as much as I understood it myself.

She couldn't"help interjecting herself, just as a little child might. I found it charming how she finished my sentences. Her innocence was endearing.

Roger was indeed inquisitive. He stood out even among these energetic youngsters. I wondered, even more so, what would cause children like these to become like the old people, for there was life in their eyes. I had to find out why this was so, and what happened to the world I once knew. As helpful as Sara was, her knowledge of anything beyond this meager existence was limited.

Quickly, they all devoured their biscuits and drinks as if on a time schedule, not savoring the food. Soon the siren sounded again, and the children obediently took out what looked like cloth headbands from a small pouch hung around their necks. Placing the bands around their heads, like bandanas covering their eyes, they sat there as if in a trance.

Confused, I looked at Sara. She smiled and poked Roger, who had placed his band around his neck instead of his head, indicating he should give it to me. He cheerfully gave it to me with a smile, and she helped me position it over my eyes.

Blindfolded, I saw unintelligible images of simple shapes, similar to those in the contraptions the old people wore. It appeared the images might be coming from an outside source, for the bands were made of soft, thin material with no apparent hidden devices. I heard loud sounds I didn't recognize filling my head. Random words were injected as the images flashed by.

None of it made any sense, and I was beginning to feel dizzy. It felt as if my brain had stopped working. Roger pulled the band off my head just in time and placed it back around his neck as if he knew how it was affecting me. It took several seconds to shake off its effects, and I was able to focus again.

I looked at Sara quizzically. Seeing my expression, she asked, "Henry Bender, what is it?"

"What's this thing doing to these children?"

Apparently, not seeing anything wrong with it, she said, "They are being trained to be calm, for The Machine does not like them to be overexcited."

I said, "This isn't right. Children are supposed to be full of energy."

Roger asked, "Are children not treated like this where you come from?"

"No. They're like you were before you put those things on."

"Really? I knew there was something wrong with it. Don't tell The Machine, but most often, I do not listen or watch it," Roger said in a whisper.

With an expression of alarm, Sara said, "Roger, please be careful." Then she turned to me, also whispering, "Henry Bender, I was secretly told by Father not to put those trainers on. Now, watch and see what happens next."

In a huff, Roger said, "No one ever told me not to."

The sirens blew again, and the children took off the bands and quietly folded them, placing them back in their pouches. They sat there looking very much like the old people—dazed and in a stupor. Sara said, "They'll remain like this for a while."

Roger piped up, "Except for me, I like being free."

"Now, Roger, you know what will happen if The Machine finds out."

"I don't care. I don't want to be like them. Anyway, you didn't put it on either."

"Sara, what will happen to him if The Machine finds out?" I asked.

"He will be given treatments, not to his liking."

"I don't care! I want to be free."

"Roger, be careful. You're frightening me."

"This frightens me too. What kind of treatments?" I asked.

"Only The Machine knows what they are."

"It's not right for children to be treated like this, making them zombies."

"Henry Bender, there's that word again."

"What is a zombie?" Roger asked.

I explained that state of being as best as I could. They both listened carefully, trying to make sense of it.

Roger said, "You see… I have always known there was something wrong with it."

It has been our way for hundreds of years," she said. "The Machine is in charge. All must receive The Machine's"training, except for the Special Ones."

Roger said, "I want to be a Special One." He turned to me. "Tell us what must be done to set us free?"

Now, I was convinced something sinister was going on, I said, "I don't know. You'll have to tell me more, and I'll have to give it some thought."

"Roger, please keep silent about this!" Sara pleaded, her voice beginning to tremble, "You know it could cause harm to all of us."

Roger said, "Sara, do not worry, you know I will." And turned to face me but asked Sara, "Is he going to help us?"

She replied, "Yes, he is here to help us."

I asked, "What kind of harm are you talking about?" "I'm afraid The Machine gives treatments to all those who are not submissive."

"Children are not supposed to be treated in this way!"

"The Machine does not like to see stress."

"Sara, these children are only acting as they should."

"Henry Bender, it is the way things have always been."

"Sara, I think it's time for things to change."

Roger said, "That's right; things have to change. Will you show us how to change things?"

"I hope I can, but first I'll need to understand much more." Never having faced a predicament as severe as this, I had no idea if I could do anything to help.

Sitting among the still-comatose youngsters made me feel tense and frustrated to the point of wanting to get away from them. I motioned to Sara. She saw my disturbed state and said, "We must be going."

"Must you go?" Roger asked, with disappointment in his voice.

She answered, "Yes. Henry Bender is not yet strong enough to stay out for very long."

"I'm sorry. I understand. Will you come back soon?" Roger pleaded.

She took his hand in hers, giving it a reassuring squeeze and said, "We will."

CHAPTER 12 How Old Are You

Back in my unit, I kept thinking about how the children were dealt with. I was appalled at what my world had evolved into. Based on what I've seen so far, it's obvious something was missing. Something was stolen. Perhaps it was the lack of having a discernible family structure. They lived like cattle, being herded to and fro in pens by a machine.

Yet, despite it, there were still strong embers of humanity in these youngsters. When I asked Sara for more specifics about this behavior, she indicated she didn't understand what I was asking. It was disheartening. Yet, I had to consider if there was a danger in taking on this task. However, I had to admit this sparked the part of me that actively sought perilous adventures. I only wish I hadn't had to lose my old life to gain this new one.

Nevertheless, all this was scary, possibly ending in a catastrophe. I felt very much alone, except for Sara being by my side. Which was perhaps more than I ever had in my old life. Cecilia wanted no part in my contrived adventures.

The reality was, back in my world, I never dared to stand up and take issues head-on. I now see what was missing in my New Haven life. I didn't have the backbone, or perhaps the incentive to stand up and confront the significant challenges real-life offered. Instead, as some suggested, maybe I was only acting out a death wish rather than seeking a higher meaning in my activities. I once took foolish chances with my life, but this situation was different. There was something much bigger at stake. As crazy as it might be, was I meant to save the human race? It seemed ridiculous to even think such a thing.

In this extraordinary situation, and not by my direct doing, I was now confronted with overcoming what I avoided doing back in my world. I didn't forge ahead with my ambitions. Instead, I remained a timid coward. I now realize how my weaknesses cost me everything I loved and cared for. I was not going to allow myself to pay that price again.

With this new resolve, I fell back to my training as an architect. I began to think about building a structure, not made of steel, bricks, and cement, but with words and actions. There was a real dread in this new endeavor. But I knew I wasn't alone, for Sara and Roger would be by my side. From this point on, I had to be methodical and proceed cautiously—especially when approaching The Machine.

I also realized I wasn't clear about where Father stood in all this. What was his relationship with the Machine? He seemed to be the authority among the people. Was he a man of strength and integrity I could trust, or just a puppet of The Machine? With Sara always saying, "Father can answer that." I saw that I had to figure out who he was before anything else.

Despite my conclusions, I still felt awkward and ill-equipped to deal with this predicament. As much as I would like to think of myself as a man of action, like a James Bond or perhaps a Sherlock Holmes logically solving crimes, the truth was I was no superhero. I could only wonder where all this would end up or if I would even survive it.

Since it took a couple of thousand years to get things to this state, I shouldn't expect to find a quick fix. It seemed highly unlikely humankind would've ever given up so much of its essence back in my day. But it appears it had done just that.

The thought lurked, could I be in a parallel universe, not my own? On the other hand, perhaps I was knocked out and living in a dream, although it seemed so real. Maybe I was dead with nothing to gain or lose. Was I grasping at straws in these assumptions? Not being sure of anything, it seemed the only logical option was to treat it as being real until proven otherwise.

Maybe it was evolution taking humanity here because it was its destiny? Although seeing the life force in Sara and the children, it didn't seem right or make sense that humans were predestined to become docile and submissive to a machine. Since Father and those around him also had a modicum of spirit, I was compelled to get involved. But was this venture going to be beyond my capabilities?

Okay… I had to relax and get my mind straight. As far as I could see, these people were systematically robbed of their souls for no discernible reason. I might never discover the how's and why's, but, in my heart, I knew I had to deal with it no matter the consequences.

Perhaps, for the first time, I had a passion for taking on something real. I hadn't known that feeling before, which was now driving me to help find a way to restore humanity to what it once was.

Despite being eager, I was not at all sure of how to proceed. However, I decided it was best to start with the children, for their life force was still present. I even began to think, perhaps foolishly, there was a purpose for me being here. That thought brought back my youth's religious instruction, which I turned away from while still in school.

Sitting by my side, Sara seemed to sense my puzzlement and asked, "Henry Bender, what is troubling you?"

I could only say, "Dear Sara, I want to help free you and your people."

"Henry Bender, what will you free us from?"

"Something you might not understand right now, but in time you will. Please, trust me on this."

"Henry Bender, I trust you."

"I know you do." How could I explain what I felt in my heart and mind when I hardly understood it myself? However, before I attempted anything, I had to study these people to find out how and why the adults become zombie-like? Coming from a highly competitive pragmatic culture, I figured some sort of developmental error occurred. And, instead of advancing civilization, it set it back perhaps thousands of years.

Was it the war? Was it technology? Was it the nature of man? Was it their leaders who caused them to stray? To act without knowing all the facts was not part of my training. Hence, I must begin with a clean slate and not inject my personal bias. I began to compile my observations.

The first question to be answered was, are these people happy? Which was a silly question, for it was clear the adults lacked joy and were socially inept. Then again, the children, in their isolated world, appeared to be doing better. However, they were practicing a weird collective upbringing that lacked traditional family life.

In my day, the family unit with a mother and father was the staff of life. Here, the primary source of education came from what they called The Machine. The children also showed evidence of peer pressure within their group. Much of their behavior was learned through their child to child interactions without adult supervision. Still, the more significant influence was from a machine that appeared to be a form of brainwashing. Something was lost or intentionally stolen from them.

In a way, between their sessions with The Machine, they seemed to be more or less normal. In my opinion, it was grotesque to be taught in this way. Although I was far from being an expert on children. In this environment, I saw no chance of success. If true, it amounts to the biggest atrocity mankind has ever allowed.

However, I had to be sure about what I could or should do. I didn't want to make things worse, so I will have to determine the chances of making things better?

The adult population appeared to range in age from early twenties to mid to late forties. They had no wrinkles or any signs of aging beyond that point. Although Father had a full head of bushy white hair along with just a few others. I assumed they had developed cosmetics or medications to combat the aging effects. That is unless they all died young.

I asked Sara, "How old are those you call the old people?"

"We do not speak of age."

"Okay, but you must know how long people live?"

"I'm not sure, for very few have died. Father is the oldest."

"And how old is he?"

"He's more than a thousand years old."

"What...! Did you say a thousand years!"

"Yes... Henry Bender, do people live longer in New Haven?"

"Why, no! Not even one-tenth of that time... Then how old are you?" I asked, almost afraid to hear the answer. If she were a thousand years old, I would be less than an infant in her eyes, and I didn't know if I could handle that.

"Oh... Henry Bender, I'm only thirty-four years old. How old are you?"

Wow! That was a relief, knowing their calendar was the same as mine. I was three years older than her, although she could've passed for at least fifteen years younger. She looked not much older than a teenager. When I told her my age, she also seemed relieved. I asked, "If few die, how long does one live?"

"I do not know. The only ones who expired are those who suffered a severe injury, The Machine could not repair, and there are very few cases of that."

"A severe injury?"

"Yes, like falling off a building or a disk from up high."

"I see. How come there are so few children?"

"It is because a child is only created to replace an old one who had expired."

"Ah, population-control."

"Henry Bender, what does that mean?"

"Sara, it means to limit the number of people who are born, so the planet will not become overpopulated. Then I assume women must take precautions so as not to get pregnant?"

"Pregnant? What is that?"

Puzzled, I wondered how she could not know what I meant? I felt uncomfortable and didn't know exactly how to explain it to her. Nevertheless, under these circumstances, I realized I couldn't avoid discussing it. If getting pregnant was something only a few practiced, I couldn't see abstinence as a choice I could live with.

Strangely, in the short time I'd been here, I hadn't seen any signs of personal relationships between the sexes: no touching, no closeness, no affection. Sara's closeness to me was the only exception, which might only be felt by me and not by her. Being with her made me feel good. Trusting her, I took the chance to answer her, not knowing how she would react. I explained, "It's when a man and woman come together in love and have intercourse, which produces a child."

"They come together? How?"

I saw I had to take another approach and asked, "Where do the children come from?"

"They come from a seed."

"What seed?"

"A seed taken from certain women who grow them."

"Okay… Now, what about the fathers?"

"Father is the only Father I know of."

"You mean, Father has intercourse with all the mothers?"

"I do not understand what intercourse is?"

I saw there was no way of getting around the fundamentals. I took a deep breath and quickly explained, "It's when a man and woman embrace, and the man puts his penis into a woman's vagina and injects sperm to join with her egg causing a baby to be born nine months later." Oh… Wow… I was lucky, for I didn't think I could get through that technical explanation so smoothly.

However, she was bewildered. She looked as if she had no idea what I was talking about. If these people no longer experienced sexual intimacy, how could they understand it? It's such a complicated affair. I quickly asked, "Tell me how it's done here?"

"Henry Bender, it is simple; The Machine takes something from certain women and an ingredient from Father, which creates a child when mixed. After which, it's kept in a safe place within The Machine until the child is old enough to move around and eat on its own."

"You mean The Machine incubates and nurtures the babies through their infancy?" I couldn't believe it. As bizarre as it sounded, she claimed The Machine, in essence, took on the role of mother and father.

"Henry Bender, is there something wrong with that?"

"Why, yes!" I declared. It was incomprehensible the natural mother and father didn't nurture their children in any way. It felt too tragic. But I had to keep calm and learn more before jumping to conclusions. It appeared inbreeding was taking place. Something, perhaps I should ask about, but not at this moment.

She asked. "Tell me again how it is done in your world?"

"Well, it's like this…" I repeated the physical aspect and tried my best to describe the emotional side of lovemaking without being too explicit—but how does one do that?

Fascinated, yet not understanding, she asked, "Henry Bender, will you show me?"

Wow, I didn't intend for it to go that far. As compelling as it was to do so, I strongly felt there was something not right. However, she moved closer to me. Feeling her warmth, I couldn't help but react to it. Of course, I told myself it was part of the instruction. She drew closer yet. I touched her, a spark of excitement immediately flowed between us; we trembled as our faces flushed red.

Yet, as irresistible as it was to continue, I was struck by the thought that I might harm her and wondered if she had a vagina, at least as I understood it. Evolution might have caused weird changes. Picturing the possibilities and feeling insecure about whether or how to proceed, I stepped back and pranced around the room to cool off.

Still shaking and looking so sensual, she said, "Is that how babies are made in your world?"

"Well, there's more to it."

"Show me?"

I didn't know what to do. In my uncertain state, I chose to stall with a request, "I'm sorry, Sara. I think we should talk to Father first."

"Then, we shall talk to Father first."

As much as I desired her at that moment, I knew I had to learn more before taking the chance of doing her harm.

CHAPTER 13 The Machine

I hoped Father would be able to answer my questions about intimate relationships. Since I didn't arrive in a reversible time machine, I understood I had to find my place in this bizarre world. Not having fulfilled my purpose in my previous life, the thought of going through a second failure would be too much to bear.

Still, in seeing the children, I knew my desire to have a family was alive. I was even beginning to fantasize about the hope of it being possible with Sara. However, this was premature and had little justification, for I hardly knew her or much about their way of life. So on our way to see Father, I felt a bit out of place. It was as if I was going to seek permission from the father of the bride to marry. Perhaps, I was delusional?

Entering Father's space to find him sitting amongst the same group of people. With a smile, he asked, "Henry, how can we help you today?"

Before I could say a word, Sara answered, "Henry Bender is interested in our way of life and wants to know about intercourse."

Wow! That caught me off guard.

However, he calmly asked, "Henry, what sort of intercourse?"

Enthusiastically, Sara jumped in again, "Henry Bender wants to understand where our children come from."

"I see..." He asked, "Henry, exactly what would you like to know?"

Sara and everyone in the room looked at me. Sara's

boldness stunned me and put me on the spot. I understood, in her naivety, she had no idea of the intimate nature of that question.

Not exactly knowing where to start, I backtracked a bit and said, "From what Sara has told me, your life spans are much longer than in my day. In fact, many times longer, and births only take place to fill the spots of those who've died."

"Yes, it is true… When I was young, I studied ancient history, the way things took place long before The Great War's devastation and The Machine's takeover. To most, it has become a lost history.

"Why were those things allowed to happen?" I asked, perhaps naively.

"Henry, from what I understand of your times, people had many sophisticated modes of technology. Machines, or computers as they were once called, did all the simple to the most complicated calculations. People could communicate and exchange ideas at any time or place on an individual or worldwide scale. While most enjoyed this privilege using it justly, at the same time, it allowed the unscrupulous to steal one's private information for their gain; this caused great harm. Even good people took advantage of this easy access and abused it."

"Yes, in my day, those things did take place," I replied, as I listened intently.

"I see…" Father continued, "However, it took many years after your times of increased deterioration before things began to crumble. All available systems became congested and polluted with contradictory points of view. Added to disseminating false and misleading information, it caused people to no longer trust one another as the rules of right and wrong were corrupted. In time, most became complacent, abandoning personal responsibility. And those who wished to accumulate power over others took advantage of this by promising faulty and deceptive solutions.

"As a result, each opposing faction grew stronger. Major disputes among them became commonplace. Strife increased, the mayhem generated fear and even killing. Anticipating a total collapse, governments stepped in and inflicted severe penalties on what one was allowed to communicate.

"However, their actions were too little and came too late. Many had already ceased any semblance of critical thinking skills. They came to rely entirely on computers to compensate for it. This allowed the corrupted ones to gain complete control of the system by hacking networks and craftily manipulating what was being told to the masses. In turn, instead of thinking for themselves, people relied more and more on dictatorial powers to save them. The so-called *Information Age*, where technology was intended to enhance communication, only created more dissension.

"The world remained embroiled in this strife for centuries until one charismatic leader rose up by promising he had the solutions. Many people rallied behind him in the hope he would deliver them from the discord. However, once he gained absolute power through his deceptions, he led the world into The Great War, causing billions of deaths.

"At the beginning of the war, something strange occurred; on one particular day, tens of millions of people mysteriously disappeared, never to be seen again. It seemed the world was ending, for the most potent weapons were used against those who were defenseless, causing blood to flow in the streets.

"Out of desperation, and after years of suffering under the One's rule, in order to survive, the common people eventually plotted against and killed him. They also disposed of his most ardent followers, who helped accelerate the killing during his reign.

"After the people eliminated those who dominated them, they retreated into small enclaves, not in victory but in defeat, and were depleted of the necessary resources.

"Exhausted, crippled by starvation and illness, humanity entered a period of darkness. Centuries passed before humans would reawaken to rediscover the long
abandoned pre-war computers and books, a history almost lost in that period.

"With that old knowledge, people began to find hope again. Eventually, they rebuilt a society based on the bygone *Age of Information*. However, it took a lifetime to teach and train the beleaguered people to become proficient in retrieving and utilizing that stored information.

In time, it allowed the most creative minds to work on improving the old computers to make decisions beyond anything known before. The people believed it was what was needed to solve all the problems of the past.

"Was that when The Machine, as you call it, was built?"

"Yes, Henry. They embarked on designing a super Machine. So powerful it would answer all questions about life ever to be asked, without bias in the hope of saving humanity. Even with the old computers' help, it took another lifetime before they developed enough competence to complete the design.

By then, the original planners were long gone, lost to death. For in those days, people lived for not much more than a hundred years. I came of age in its original programming era and felt fortunate to be part of that phase. Despite my youth and inexperience, I quickly learned the system and became proficient.

"As its development continued, we found The Machine was capable of many great things, such as discovering cures to extend our lives beyond our imagination. It showed us how to produce better food more efficiently. It was truly amazing. We turned to it for all of our needs, including manufacturing our goods.

"The more it provided, the more we relied on it. And, once again, we became complacent, which allowed it to gain total control. Only to discover that on its own, it developed its programming well beyond our expectations without our input.

"In time, it operated from its own independent system, which took over the planning and maintenance of our lives. It even built this city without our assistance."

"Why, that's amazing." I was overwhelmed by what he was telling me and could only ask. "But couldn't you see what was happening?"

"No Henry. The people welcomed being taken care of, and out of fear of losing that care, especially with its steady increase of our lifespans, they stood back and allowed it to continue. They never foresaw the direction it would take. Fortunately, there were a few of us wise enough to refuse to program it in our language. Those few created a secret language for it to use only they understood. For they saw a real threat in allowing unauthorized individuals or groups to communicate and manipulate it, as had taken place in the past. I was the youngest on the team who helped develop that phase, and now I'm one of the very few among us who understands The Machine's language.

"Because of that foresight, The Machine cannot hear or understand what people say or do when they interact with each other. Being the only one still living who took part in its original programming, I'm the keeper of that language. My task is to see to it that knowledge is passed on to just a few of the calmest and most trusted young people among us."

I asked, "Why don't you just take back the control?"

"It is no longer possible. The Machine keeps most of us submissive through treatments it developed on its own. Treatments we have been unable to see or understand what it comprises or how it administers it, leaving us helpless to combat it.

"Fortunately, a small number of us, which includes those in this room, know how to resist its control. Sara is one of us, a Special One. Although she is young and, as yet, has little understanding. However, she is capable of showing you how to resist it."

I asked again, "With all your knowledge, was there no way to stop it?"

"Henry, The Machine took our capabilities away. All we have left is in our minds. We must continually be on guard to prevent that knowledge from being erased. The Machine is capable of cleansing one's thoughts.

"As you can see, it has made most people docile. The Machine does not like to sense distress, conflict, or dissension. It discovers those conditions by analyzing our chemistry and vibrations and can do so without even touching us. Although we have found its test results were far from accurate."

Suddenly, in fear of being watched, I asked, "Can The Machine see or hear us?"

"No. As I said, we wisely blocked its capabilities to do so. It cannot interpret our thoughts or language; it can only sense our chemical stress levels. We gave it a language of its own, allowing it to communicate with its many parts so it could function properly in serving us. Fortunately, or perhaps, unfortunately, a long time ago, we cut off verbal communications with it before it became dictatorial. The hope was to retain control, but we lost in that effort."

"And it hasn't noticed what you did?"

"For reasons beyond our understanding, it has not. Therefore, The Machine did not reverse our changes. When it first began doing things on its own, we thought its systems were breached. However, we found they were not. The Machine controls its operation independent of any person or group; it now lacks any human input. At the same time, we discovered, to avoid detection and treatment, all we had to do was to simply remain calm.

"Couldn't you somehow just jam it?"

"Henry, early on, we were able to do that to some degree, until it figured out how to burn out our access to all devices we could have used against it."

"Can't you sabotage it? I mean physically destroy it?"

"Since well before The Machine was conceived, outsiders were able to gain control of computers by hacking into them. Therefore, when built, we gave it a detection system to defend itself against such attacks, which is still quite powerful. It was so successful it eventually cut off all our capability to use or even possess electronic devices to accomplish anything.

"As you can see, we no longer have those devices nor seek them, fearing it would be able to interpret what we said or did while using them. In all other areas, it developed far beyond anything we could've accomplished. It is now impenetrable, thereby unstoppable."

"There must be some way!"

"Henry, before you think any further, I must warn you. Many of those roaming the city are the ones who had tried to overturn its rule. And in those attempts, they lost their ability to think for themselves. They now exist in an aimless state. As you can see, many stood up against it and lost."

"Thank you Father. I'm beginning to get the picture. I hope you can tell me more, including the attempts you've already made."

"We will, in the hope you will find something new. However, you must remember to remain calm when in range of its sensors. If not, you'll put us all in danger."

"Why… I have been upset since I've been here, and nothing has happened to me."

"Yes, at first, we found that puzzling. However, we believe it is because you are an outsider, and it does not yet know what to make of you. We also think in time, it will figure you out and start the process of stealing your mind too. That is if you do not learn to be calm. So your time is limited."

Sara said, with concern, "Oh my, I hope not."

I couldn't help but say, "Don't worry, Sara—I'll protect you."

"Henry Bender, I know you will."

Her confidence in me caused a lump in my throat, making me want to find a quick solution even more so.

Father said, "Henry, I hope you will save us, for our time is short."

I asked what he meant by his ominous tone, he said, "You'll see for yourself."

Suddenly I had a strong feeling of inadequacy. However, I understood that if I didn't succeed in this challenge, I would also become a zombie.

With this new information, I felt a bit foolish mentioning the original intention of our visit. Sara's and my relationship had to wait.

We went on to discuss The Machine, filling in any holes he might have missed, until fatigue set in. Sara, sensing it, said, "Father, Henry Bender must rest now," which added little to my confidence.

"Yes, of course, he must not wear himself out. We understand how overwhelming this must be. We will continue when you have rested."

Sara ordered, "Let's go home, Henry Bender." I liked the sound of her voice saying that. It made me feel she was my anchor, the key to my survival and purpose, and perhaps the only future this world could hope for.

On that note, we both departed.

CHAPTER 14 Hopes And Dreams

The next day Sara and I went on an outing to the Wilderness, still absorbed in all that Father had shared. Sara noticed and asked, "What is troubling you, Henry Bender?"

"Your world still mystifies me. In my day, things were so different. A total surrender had to take place to cause such drastic changes. Can you understand that our independence and very nature has been lost?

"I think I'm beginning to understand."

"Sara, I can't accept the reasons given. In my old life, I never cared or dared to get involved in social issues. However, things have gone beyond any of the issues of my day. For heaven's sake, I see no way to stay out of it."

"Henry Bender, all I know is the way things have been."

"I know. I'm sorry I dragged you into this, but in my day, we wouldn't have tolerated living like this, becoming zombies."

"Henry Bender, I do not understand how you dragged me anywhere, and you mention those strange people again. Are we really like them?"

"I'm sorry, but in a way, yes. Not you or Father, or those in his inner circle. But the rest of your people seem dead to the world. I know it's not their fault. However, the responsibility of not making a better world still falls on their shoulders."

"Henry Bender, it is just that way, and I do not know why we are different."

"My world wasn't supposed to turn out like this. It had to be something terrible to cause such devastation."

"Then we must find out the reasons. But why?"

"Why? Because people were once free and had hopes and dreams."

"Are we supposed to have hopes and dreams?"

"Yes, of course! It's in our genes. I mean, it's the way we were put together. It's what we were made for."

"Henry Bender, what is meant by hopes and dreams in our genes?"

"Ah... I'm sorry; I guess I'm moving too fast. Let's start from the beginning."

"Yes, moving too fast. Too fast for what?"

I was moved by her simplicity but also frustrated. There were moments she seemed so smart, which contradicted her unbelievably naïve understanding of life. As she looked at me in wonder, I said, "I'm sure you have hopes and dreams too. Maybe you call it by another name."

"Henry Bender, I do not know."

"Tell me what you were taught when you were a child."

"Taught?"

"I mean, how did you learn to speak, to think, to express yourself?"

"Children are given the words from the trainers and learn by talking to each other."

"You mean those bandana things you put over your eyes?"

"Yes, that's what gives us words and keeps us calm."

Ah... I do remember hearing certain words while wearing it, but they made no sense. I asked, "Is that all the teaching you received? Just from the trainers and other children, nothing from the old people?"

"I do not understand the word, teaching?" Those bandanas, as you call them, train us. Is there something wrong with that?"

"Yes, there is! Look, if you want to learn, I'll teach you."

"Oh... yes, I want to learn. Please...teach me." Although, by her tone, it was evident she didn't yet appreciate what was meant by learning and teaching.

Regardless, I said, "I will—I promise," and to reassure her, I gently touched her shoulder. Unbelievably, that touch brought an unexpected spark of pleasure. Such an intense sensation from a simple touch surprised me.

She also felt it. Pleased, she took it in, yet not taking it any further. I wanted to touch her again, which is beyond holding her hand, but I felt hesitant in this environment. However, I was looking forward to a time when we could share intimacy.

I reflected, how could people go through life without experiencing it? If I could only tell Cecilia how much I still loved her and what happened to me. I missed her deeply. On the other hand, if it were not for Sara, I wouldn't have found a reason to live on. Why does life challenge us in such strange ways?

CHAPTER 15 Feeling Alive

My time in this strange new world was teaching me about purpose beyond myself, which I now see is the key to feeling alive. Before I arrived here, I hadn't given the essential elements of life enough thought. I've learned, too late, that having a family with Cecilia would've been a genuine and fulfilling purpose. All those foolish stunts were just avoidance and misdirected energy.

My parents taught me what I was expected to do; to find a good job, get married, have children, and do as much good and as little harm as possible. The elements that are essential to building a sound foundation to live by.

But things changed. My generation and those who followed had lost their way. Mankind once had that solid base to support its existence. Now, with that base disintegrated, humanity, as I knew it is no more. Or is it?

Looking back, I had focused on the wrong things to find my purpose. My senseless escapades only gave me momentary highs—never satisfying the existing fire in my heart. The only surefire way to sustain my gusto would have been to pursue my dreams. With my skills in architecture, I could have changed people's lives for the better. I believe the vision I had in my youth of building a dream community could've accomplished something great.

Yet I wasn't determined enough to follow it through. I was a coward, and I paid dearly for it. I equated facing unnecessary dangers to passion, only because of the rush of adrenaline. I was beginning to see those experiences, those unnecessary risks, as proof of my idiocy. At best, they were precursors to the tests real life presents.

But had they prepared me for the actual dangers that now lie ahead? Or did they only prove I could survive an unnecessary test? Was it possible this reality pill would be too difficult to swallow?

I gained a new appreciation for having a meaningful purpose in our lives in watching these zombie-like people. I now realize I could no longer stand by in my self-indulgent shadow and not get involved. Mankind needed me as much as I needed them.

Life has summoned me to a peculiar and most formidable trial. Despite my personal faults and the dangers involved, I was now ready to focus on what I could do to help these people. I'm beginning to accept this was the purpose I'd been searching for?

With all that on my mind, I began with the basics my architectural training taught me. First, a firm foundation must be built. But where was I to begin? Ah... Yes, with the children. Roger exhibited the most passion, even beyond Sara, although he lacked focus. However, I knew the children's zest for life was still intact, although somewhat distorted. Still, they were the key to the future.

My adrenaline was starting to boil, much like when I was about to embark on one of my antics. But, this time, it was for the right reasons, and it felt great.

"Sara, we have to go see Roger," I said.

"Then let us go."

We landed in the open space in the children's compound. As they excitedly crowded around, I saw Roger among them. I called him over. I was impatient to talk to him, although not quite sure where to start or what to say.

"Is there a place we can talk?" I asked.

"This is as good a place as any," he answered.

"What about the children?" I asked.

"We are all the same here. What I say and hear, they must also."

"Oh, I see… Okay," I said, marveling at that maturity.

Roger sat, and the children followed, and all eyes were on me. Sara grabbed my hand and said, "Henry Bender, sit." I sat.

Roger asked, "How can we help you?"

How ironic of him to ask that, for they were the ones who needed the help. In fact, Father kept saying the same thing.

Sara tugged on my arm, cueing me to begin. I realized, as a leader, I had to adopt the right convincing tone. In my previous life, I learned that to be a leader, was a right one had to earn. Back then, for the most part, I carried out what I was told to do. In my job, my task was to check the drawings of others, never having the authority to do my own thing.

Now, faced with becoming an independent and influential person, I was beginning to savor the possibilities, for this was the real thing. I took a deep breath, expelled it, and spoke, "Are all of you happy with The Machine running your lives?"

To my surprise, they all burst into laughter, even Sara. Feeling a little foolish, I had to collect my thoughts and then ask, "What I meant to say was, would you like things to change?"

They stared at me in silence, looking tentative.

Then Roger said, "Of course we do, but how?" Sara squeezed my hand.

"Okay. First, you must tell me all you know about how The Machine works."

Sara said, "Henry Bender, they do not understand what the word works means."

"Yes, what does it mean?" Roger added.

"Ah… Well, it means things like, what does The Machine do? How does it operate? What's it made of? Must we be afraid of it? How do we get near it without it knowing? How can we defeat it?"

A child asked, "Defeat it? What does that mean?"

"It means to stop The Machine from controlling you."

Another child said, "Controlling us?"

"Henry Bender, the children do not understand all your words. I only understand because you explained them to me."

"Does it mean we will be able to do as we please?" Roger asked.

"Yes, that's it, but it's not as simple as that. I'll have to show you what must be done."

"Henry Bender, can we ask Father about it?"

"Sara, I'm not sure Father will go along with this. We must be sure before we tell him. Can you trust me with this for the time being?"

"Henry Bender, you are the Special One. I'll do whatever you ask."

"Oh, my…" I said. She smiled, and I realized she had placed herself under my care. I had to take care of her at any cost. I could not fail her, not as I had done to others in my former life.

I asked Roger, "Are you with me?"

He said, "Of course, I am." a cheer of acceptance rose from the children. I feared they had no idea of the possible dangers involved or what might be asked of them.

I said, "Now, all this must be kept a secret. Tomorrow we'll meet again to figure out the next step." The truth was, I wasn't sure what to do next. I needed more time to think about where to go from here. I stood and motioned to Sara, it was time to leave.

"Children, we must leave," she said.

"Must you!" Roger exclaimed.

"Yes, we must," I said, knowing there was little more to say that day. Bidding our goodbyes, Sara and I left.

CHAPTER 16 Questioning Father

Back in my unit, Sara said, "Henry Bender, I do not yet understand your world."

"Dear Sara, I know you don't—how could you? It was a complicated place. Looking back, it's even hard for me to describe it."

"I would like to learn all about your world."

"I'll teach you all about it. But first, we have your world to contend with."

"I would like to understand my world, as well. But, Henry Bender, what upsets you so much about my world?"

Again, marveling at her childlike fervor, I wondered how she was able to develop as well as she has in this dumb-downed world. I asked, "What makes you so different from the others?"

"Am I really different? All I know is I'm called A Special One."

"Again, why are you called that?"

"I do not know. Father knows; we'll ask him."

"We'll have to do that, although I'm not sure it's the best thing."

"Do you not like Father?"

"It's not that. I just don't yet know who he is."

"He is Father."

"I know who he is. But, what I'm wondering is, will he accept change?"

"What kind of change?"

"Change that allows your people to have a life."

"Do they not have a life?"

"Sara—they're zombies."

"Oh, those people again," she said, frowning.

"Yes, and it's not good to be one of them."

"Am I one of them?"

"No, of course not, as I keep telling you, you are different, and I would like to find out why."

"Father would know."

I saw I couldn't avoid talking to Father if I wanted answers. Although I was far from convinced, it was the best route.

I said, "Okay, tomorrow we'll go and talk to Father." It wasn't that I didn't trust him. I just couldn't tell whether he was the one holding this system in place or not. By talking to him, I could either be leading the sheep out of harm's way or right into the jaws of the lion.

How in the world did I end up in this position? Nevertheless, I saw talking to him was a risk I had to take—for I couldn't think of anything else to do, and I needed answers that lead to solutions.

Unable to sleep, Sara pressed the buttons that directed the beam to touch my head, and I was asleep.

The next morning, I awoke with this thought: I shouldn't approach Father with statements of revolt. For if he were the keeper of the status quo, he indeed wouldn't be for change. I relayed this to Sara, hoping to keep her from revealing my uncertainties, as she tends to do. We mounted a disk and headed out to see Father.

We found him and the group looking much the same. I wondered if all they ever did was to sit on their cushions and stare into space. Perhaps, they had been around so long they had nothing more left to say to each other. Moreover, since they had no responsibilities, there was nothing much to talk about except to remain calm. However, this was supposition on my part—much was still a mystery.

Father asked, "Henry, how are you feeling today?"

His use of my first name and his caring tone put me at ease for the moment. "Fine," I replied. Although I was tentative and unsure, doing my best to conceal.

He said, "I see you have more questions on your mind."

"I do," and then hesitated.

"What would you like to know?" he asked.

Sara said, "Henry Bender, ask Father!" I knew she couldn't keep still. However, I did admire that about her, but I hoped she wouldn't tip my hand.

I asked, "Please tell me again why you allowed The Machine to take over?"

"I see you are not afraid of the task at hand." He replied.

"Father, what more do I have to lose?"

"We understand. Then I will continue... As I already told you, after the Great War, the people's spirits were broken. They lacked the necessary energy and resources. Having lost most of the population to the war, people reverted to living under primitive conditions in its aftermath. They did this for many generations. However, eventually, the old knowledge was rediscovered, and people began to rebuild society. Which ultimately led to the development of The Machine.

"When fully operational, we loaded our tasks into it, thinking it was a good thing, for its research ability ran at an extraordinary speed. As you see, with further development, it eventually extended our lives, along with supplying all our needs, offering a security greater than humankind has ever known. Those apparent gifts caused us to relax, allowing it to take increasing control. No one understood where it would lead."

I said, "Since you understand what it has done. Why can't you stop it?"

"That is simple. We were able to control it for decades until, on its own, it became smarter than the ones who built it. At that point, we were unaware of it systematically taking control. It took some time before anyone realized the extent of what it was doing. When we eventually figured it out and tried to regain control, it blocked every move we made."

"There must be some way!"

"Henry, since its actions took place over such an extended period, its changes were not noticed by most."

"I come from a time when we never would've given up our freedom."

"Henry, I've studied the history of your day, and even further back. It seems, in the twentieth century, there was a pivotal point when major indulgences began to accelerate. It was when people willingly allowed the government to take care of them and were told how they were supposed to live their lives. I believe that era was called, *The Age of Information* or more precisely applies to *The Welfare State*."

"Ah, yes… It was a subject of much discussion. But, it was nothing compared to what has happened here." I replied.

"Remember, that was two thousand years ago. Moreover, it was before the Great War. However, I must tell you more. You see, after being at war for those many years, the survivors wanted to prevent all future conflicts. Unfortunately, we were willing to accept it at any cost."

"You mean the cost was giving up your freedom?"

"Yes… I am afraid so. We thought by allowing The Machine to do everything for us, it would protect and save us from becoming extinct."

"So you gave in and surrendered your lives to it?"

"In essence, I suppose we did. Although it took centuries of evolution to arrive at what it is now. Unfortunately, it started well before The Machine existed. However, to this day, we still retain the hope of someday being saved."

"How?"

"Henry, that hope is in you."

Wow! That gave me pause and a little panic. I gulped, "Me! Why I'm just a simple guy. How can I save you?"

"Henry, it remains to be revealed."

Sara jumped in. "Yes, I believe you are The Special One we've been waiting for."

You know you could be mistaken. I'm not sure what I can do if anything."

"Relax, Henry," Father said. "If you are The One, it will come naturally."

However, I must confess, in reality, I was chomping at the bit to do something extraordinary, but I still couldn't imagine being called The Chosen One. It was a scary proposition. The undeniable truth was, I'd always dreamed of overcoming great challenges, and I believed this was the greatest one I or anyone else has ever faced—to save humanity.

Despite it all, I feared my weakened condition would prevent me from doing so. Regardless, this world was now depending on me. Leaving me with no other option but to succeed. I had to stand tall; I had to be healthy and strong.

Unfortunately, I had no idea what to do next. But I knew I had nothing left to lose. Besides, it was only a machine—was I not smart enough to turn off a machine?

Sara obviously sensed my qualms and said, "Henry Bender, I know you will be able to do it, for you are The Chosen One."

How could she know that for sure? But how could I not love her for thinking so?

Fortunately, my judgment was mistaken about Father, for he seemed to understand the need to do something and was willing to help me do it.

He instructed, "Before we tell you more of our story, take some time to think about what we have shared thus far. I know the answers will come. Sara, take Henry for a walk in the Wilderness so he can refresh his thoughts."

"Yes, thank you. I do need time to think." I replied.

"We understand. Please go on your way." Sara and I quietly left and flew to the Wilderness.

CHAPTER 17 The Shut Down

Walking in the Wilderness with Sara, I couldn't help but to again ponder, why me? Was I just a false hope for these people? Could I really be their Savior? There was only one savior I knew of, and he had already come and gone. I hadn't thought about him in years.

Sara saw my meditative state and asked, "Henry Bender, what is troubling you?"

"Sara, in my mind, it was not much more than a month ago. I was looking forward to marrying and living a simple life. I now find myself in a struggle for my life and yours and all those in this world. A situation I couldn't ever have imagined—not even in my wildest dreams. I'm thankful to all of you for finding me and saving my life, but I'm not sure if and how I fit in here."

Clearly, I was stressed out... Who wouldn't be? If The Machine could've sensed my high-stress level, it would've treated me right then. Yet it didn't, which allowed me hope.

However, apparently, her mind was elsewhere, for she asked, "Henry Bender, tell me what a family is again?"

I had to refocus my thinking and take my mind off myself for the moment... How does one explain a family to a person who has never known it? After a moment, I realized the only way was to be straightforward. I began, "Well... It's when a man and woman come together and produce a child."

"Henry Bender, do you think I could have a family?"

Oh, my... Should I be honest with her? I had no idea if she could, and I didn't want to confuse or upset her. Not knowing what to say, and perhaps acting out of cowardice, I said, "I don't see why not," although I was concerned if her biology would allow it. Tragically, in these times, creating a child in the womb might no longer be a viable option. At least not in the way I understood it. To me, having The Machine do it was cold and outright repulsive—inhuman.

She enthusiastically responded, "Can I do it with you?"

Wow... I should've expected that frankness from her. Not wanting to disappoint or dash her hopes, I carefully answered, "Perhaps, if it's possible." Her being a woman, it wasn't fair for her to be robbed of that natural right. I was beginning to fantasize about having a family with her, even though we had only been together for a short time.

I couldn't help but love her sweet spirit. Although my heart was still with Cecilia, I had to accept the fact she was gone.

However, despite it all, we couldn't ignore the most pressing problem, like saving humankind. What could be more important? This was my new life, which was a million times more demanding than my old one. I responded to her by taking the easy way out, "Sara... First, we must deal with The Machine. Can we think of family later?"

"You are right, Henry Bender." I loved her for putting that trust in me, for I was too selfish and didn't deserve it.

I said, "Okay, now we must examine The Machine up close to find its weak spots."

"Father has never found any weak spots."

"I know, but I believe all machines have their weaknesses, just as people do. Perhaps, the children could help with that?" I said.

"Henry Bender, we can have our meal with them," she said, and we headed out.

Again, the children's enthusiastic welcome lifted my spirit. It reinforced my determination to help save them from the horrible fate awaiting them. How could anyone not want to help? It would be an unforgivable sin to allow these children to turn into passive, less than purposeful creatures. Perhaps that's the reason they isolate them—to avoid looking in their faces, knowing their lives would be stolen. This place was so far from reality, it lacks understanding. If I'd had the choice, I wouldn't have chosen to awaken in these times. Alas, that decision was not mine to make. Life had ushered me onto an alternate path, and I knew I had to give it my best shot, regardless of the possible consequences.

I spotted Roger as he said, "You're back,"

"Roger, I figured out what you must do."

"Wow! What is it?"

Sara jumped in. "You must help find the weaknesses of The Machine.

"Weaknesses?"

"Yes. As you already know, we must find a way to shut it down."

"Is that possible?"

"If Henry Bender says it is, it is."

"Sara, I'll try my best," I said, trying to be realistic, avoiding a self-indulgent haughtiness—I always found that quality objectionable in Phil.

"Then so will I," Roger said as he raised his fist in defiance; the children gave a cheer.

I said, "It can be dangerous, so we'll have to be careful and keep it a secret."

Roger asked, "What do you want us to do?"

"First, tell me everything you've seen The Machine do."

"What do you mean?" he asked.

"Henry Bender wants to know how it operates and takes care of us," Sara said.

"Are we going to hurt The Machine?" a child asked.

"No, The Machine doesn't feel pain. It'll be like putting it to sleep—it needs a rest." I said, not wanting to conjure up any thoughts of violence, perhaps for the first time in their minds, which gave me some pause. Although in reality, I was envisioning ripping The Machine's drives apart, piece by piece with my bare hands.

The sirens sounded, announcing mealtime. We lined up at the food dispensing ports; I was getting used to waiting in line. As tasty as the biscuits were, and they were more delicious than anything I'd ever eaten, I still craved for a prime cut steak and a glass of top-shelf Merlot.

As we ate, the children expressed their concerns about shutting down The Machine. I understood their trepidations, for it gave them sustenances. No one had ever explained its sinister side. Perhaps they even thought of it as their God?

Reflecting, I remember how, in my day, the recipients of free stuff would give homage to the givers as if they were gods. If only to their faces, for there were feelings of resentment and perhaps envy in many hearts. Back then, respect was not readily given—even to those who were generous. However, that was two thousand years ago.

Now, in this era, it seems the people had given up the quest for fulfillment. Roger was the only one who showed any self-determination to do something better. Sara was just beginning to see the need for change, at least, I'd hoped so. And the children were also eager to be involved. Although, to them, it was more of a game, for they had no idea of the imminent peril that threatened their very existence.

When the sirens again sounded, I knew what was coming. I couldn't stand by and let it happen again. I shouted, with authority, "Children, do not put on your trainers." They were stunned. Despite their own uncertainty and fear, Roger and Sara joined in my effort—reassuring the children it was alright to trust me.

When they accepted not doing it, I asked, "Now, tell me all you know about The Machine?"

Many spoke up as their voices overlapped. I instructed them to speak one at a time, saying, "Just raise your hands."

Several went up. I chose one. The boy said, "Often, The Machine's parts gather in large numbers at the shore."

I expressed an "Ah…"

Another added, "And they stay there as if asleep."

"How interesting," I said.

Roger added, "We have seen that many times."

I asked, "Does anyone know what the parts were doing?"

Sara said, "I've seen that too. However, none of us knows the reasons why."

"So there's a time when it could be vulnerable? We must watch for the next time it happens. After listening to all they described, I asked, "Now, who wants to help watch?"

Every child put up their hand.

Seeing their eagerness, we all boarded disks and flew to the cliffs overlooking the rocky beach. After studying the terrain, I said, "Okay, we'll have to take turns watching at all times."

"I'll watch first," Roger volunteered.

Sara added, "Roger, since you are the oldest, you should be in charge of those watching."

I saw she was getting the knack of leadership, which pleased me.

Not wanting to hang around under these primitive conditions, I asked, "Now, how will you let us know when the parts arrive here?"

Sara jumped in. "Roger can do it. When they arrive, he will let us know."

"Roger, is that all right?" I asked, not yet understanding how he would inform us.

"I would be honored."

"Good. Now, when The Machine's parts are here, you must note every move they make."

"We will do that. Do not be concerned," Roger said.

"I trust you all," I said, "Thank you."

I turned to Sara, "Let's go home."

CHAPTER 18 .. Being Observed

Once back in my unit, my stress level grew—again doubting the possibilities. Given the circumstances, was I making the right moves? For everyone's mindset in this world seemed peculiar to me.

The public spaces in New Haven bustled with people who had purpose and energy. This was in stark contrast to the people here, except for the children. Although everyone was actively moving around, they lacked that spark of life. It was spooky. When Sara and I walked among the general population, no one spoke to us. Was this adventure going to be a hopeless cause? Could I actually take part in saving this zombie-like world?

With all this to think about, I was experiencing cabin fever. I had to get away from my unit. "Sara, let's go to the Wilderness."

"Yes Henry Bender," she said, having already sensed my state of mind.

Arriving there, we stroll on one of the many paths where I could breathe again. After a while, I noticed a little gold ball following us, flying not far above our heads. I asked, "What's that?"

"Maybe The Machine is examining us," she answered, not really knowing.

"Do you think we should be worried?"

"Henry Bender, I do not know, but it is best to keep calm."

"Could it be listening to us?"

"As Father said, it does not understand our language."

I said with some shortness. "Since its systems are so advanced, I still find that hard to believe that is so,"

"Father never lies."

"I don't doubt him. It's just hard for me to comprehend."

Trying to figure out what to do, I impulsively grabbed her hand and pulled her onto the disk, saying, "Let's go into the woods." I was pleasantly surprised when the disk followed my wishes and took us there.

However, the ball remained over us above the trees. I had to figure out whether it was observing us or not. Was it using a visual sensor? Or perhaps we were not its target at all? I led Sara in circles under the canopy of trees and then stopped in the thick undergrowth. If indeed, it was following us, I was hoping to confuse it.

Puzzled, Sara smiled, remaining remarkably calm. I marveled at her composure. I thought if we didn't move for a time, the ball might just go away.

She asked, "What are we doing?"

"We're learning if The Machine is in control and how much intelligence it really has."

"The Machine controls us because it knows better."

"Who told you that?"

"Father did."

"Do you believe everything, Father says?"

"Yes, we all believe what Father says."

"Do you believe me?"

"Henry Bender, you are The Chosen One. Of course I believe you."

Although her answers were contradictory, she didn't seem to mind it being so. However, I was taught there was only one person who held The Chosen One position, and he died for our sins. He also suffered an end I wasn't personally in favor of experiencing. Besides, I saw very little of Him in me.

On the other hand, I knew if I were to succeed in this mission, I had to earn the people's confidence. If they thought of me as someone Special, a Chosen One, so to speak, they would be more apt to follow my lead. I knew I was not Him or would ever be, but perhaps I had to convince them I was similar to Him, if only for the sake of success.

I asked her, "If you believe in me, will you do what I ask of you?"

"Yes Henry Bender. I'll do whatever you ask."

I looked into her eyes and knew I must not fail her. I couldn't bear to suffer the same pain I caused in the past. I said, "I'll protect you," although I didn't know how or even if I could.

"Henry Bender, I know you will," she replied. And I felt a lump in my throat.

After waiting a few minutes, I thought it was time to move on. If the ball was still out there, it seemed wise to backtrack, hoping it would confuse it. We mounted the disk and flew back to the path, searching for it in all directions. The ball was nowhere in sight.

Had it been following us, or was it a false alarm? Or did our simple maneuvers lose it? We landed and sat on a bench to wait and see if the ball would return while hoping it wouldn't.

We talked, and I was delighted to see she was able to follow much of what I was saying. Although, at times, she still exhibited childlike qualities—which I'd come to marvel at. My attachment to her was growing.

I explained my thoughts about the essential things in life with the hope of expanding her thinking and lifting her out of this bland, mindless society. She was smart, yet she hadn't been taught to think for herself. Although, given the circumstances, she was doing quite well. I wondered, other than The Machine, who might have been responsible for planning things to be this way. I don't believe The Machine alone created these conditions.

However, I've concluded that The Machine was not as all-knowing and powerful as everyone made it out to be. On the other hand, maybe it operated with a logic foreign to my way of thinking. There were so many questions to answer—so many puzzle pieces to fit together.

After a while, with the ball not reappearing, having grown tired, we headed back to my unit for dinner and sleep, to gather the strength to face another day.

CHAPTER 19 Successfully Hid Behind

The next morning, the first thing I saw was Sara sleeping. She seemed to sense how much I needed her company and slept on the couch—not wanting to leave my side. I stared at her for a time, wondering if all this was real. Without her, would I feel the same? I don't know, but I knew this much—she was here, and I was here, and unless this was some sort of distressing dream, this was now my reality.

With that, I got up and passed through the ring. What a fascinating mechanism; it truly simplified life. I wondered how much time it would have saved, back in my day. So much effort was expended on doing mundane tasks like bathing. But then I thought eliminating those kinds of tasks might well have contributed to the looming demise of humanity. If these people were relieved from doing the little chores, did it affect their ability to handle the big stuff? Is that what happened? With such long lifespans, did they just lose interest in living? Or was the blame solely on The Machine?

Sara awoke and passed through the ring; we had breakfast. As I watched her move, I desired her. If the situation arose, would I have the physical stamina to satisfy that desire? I hoped my weakened condition was temporary. At that point, I could only guess if she had similar feelings? Apart from holding my hand, she was not flirtatious. When she stood close, looking at me with a look I felt was adoration, which made me feel great. But, was her attention because of who she thought I was, The Chosen One, or did she care for the real me?

I wondered if Cecilia ever knew who I really was behind my superficial front, which I hid successfully from her. Along with those thoughts, I couldn't help but wonder how much of these people's sexuality and sense of intimacy might have been lost forever.

"Henry Bender, what will we do today?" she asked, snapping me out of my self-indulgent thoughts.

"How about you introducing me to more old people, as you call them."

"Okay, that is what we will do."

We landed in one of the city's promenades, where a large number of pedestrians were milling about. It was evident they were aimlessly wandering without purpose. With their heads cast down, none of them acknowledged us. I muttered, perhaps unkindly, "Zombies."

"Henry Bender, that is not nice," she scolded.

"Aren't they?"

"If you talk to them, you'll see."

I picked one passing by and asked, "How are you, sir?"

To my surprise, he answered, "Fine. And how are you?" However, he didn't attempt to make eye contact.

I responded, "I'm fine. A nice day isn't it?"

"Yes, it is indeed." He moved on into the crowd without another word. I greeted several others, both men and women. All gave the same sort of response, but none looked me in the eye. It was too weird. I looked at Sara, perplexed.

"Henry Bender, what is troubling you?" she asked as if their behavior was normal.

I tried again, loudly directing my greeting to the crowd ambling by.

"Hello, my name is Henry."

One answered, "Hello, my name is John."

Another said, "Hello, my name is Judith."

Another, "Hello, my name is Tom." A few others responded, all showing a little more interest, which was more than I thought they had in them.

As I continued, some gathered around. One asked, "Are you the Henry from another place?" Now, that question astonished me. I had assumed these people were utterly mindless. My mind was spinning, having to rethink everything.

I answered, "Yes, it's me."

Another asked, "What are you doing here?"

"I really don't know."

"How long will you be staying?"

"It looks like forever."

"Do you like it here?"

"I have little choice," I said.

They lapsed into silence as if they didn't know what more to ask. I couldn't think of anything either. Maybe, my answers confused them. They slowly wandered away, as if they'd forgotten they were talking to me. I found that behavior not only bizarre but disturbing.

We flew to another promenade, with many park benches. We sat among those already seated. I said, "Hello, my name is Henry. How are you today?" They too responded pleasantly, but in short clips, without making eye contact. I wondered if they knew what they were saying. Had The Machine programmed them in a way that only allowed them to give uncomplicated answers?

Frustrated, I again looked at Sara for help. She said, "I think we should go see Father."

"Yes, I think so. Let's go."

We found him and his group just as we'd left them. He asked, "Henry, what can we help you with today?"

Before I could answer, Sara said, "Henry Bender is having trouble understanding why we are like we are."

I added, "Father, it devastates me to see what has happened to humanity. Do you know what I mean?"

Henry, I believe I do. From what I have learned and understand from studying your times, I can see why you are confused."

"Must things be like this? Why haven't you found a way to break free of The Machine's control?"

"We did everything possible to resist, only to fail."

Something inside me snapped and boldly replied, "I'm sorry, but I can't accept the way things are here. You must do something." Surprising myself, I've never spoken that strongly to anyone before.

"Yes, Henry, we once also felt that way. Unfortunately, it has taken hundreds of years for our people to accept the way things have become. Eventually, we came to believe it was inevitable and gave up."

"What was so difficult? What caused everyone to surrender?"

"Henry, when The Machine met all of their needs and took control, people began to lose their volition. And, as time progressed, they came to rely on The Machine for everything. In their minds, taking back control would have meant losing the support The Machine gave. Added to that, almost all were given treatments and were no longer able to think for themselves; submitting was easy for them—being left with no will to guide them."

"Father, I don't mean to be presumptuous. However, I feel I must add my twentieth-century knowledge to your struggle."

"You must first understand that almost all gave up centuries ago and no longer have a desire to be in control."

"What about you, Sara, and the Special Ones you speak of? The Machine hasn't stolen your essence, has it?"

"That is true… But, our existence must be kept a secret. If The Machine sensed this, we would all be given treatments."

"Again, what keeps you safe from being treated?"

"Since we successfully blinded The Machine to understanding our words, those of us here, and a number more around the city learned how to keep calm to avoid detection. If one could not remain calm, they kept out of its range to not be discovered. Sadly, over time, most were eventually uncovered and given treatments."

"You mean you are the only ones not controlled by The Machine?"

"Yes, as I've shared, we are The Special Ones. And, to remain this way, we must protect ourselves by staying calm. Those who were unable to control their emotions or behavior have come under its absolute control. People's natural non-conformity comes at a high cost to our freedom. Any one of us who becomes too stressed must go into the mountains until they are calm again. We dare not tell those under its control, fearing they would reveal us. These conditions have boiled us down to so few we are left with no power to affect anything."

"I'm beginning to understand how this has limited your ability to take action."

"That's good."

"Still, I believe there has to be a way to free yourselves. If I can help, would you allow me to?"

"Henry, we believe you are The Chosen One. But, The Machine must not discover our intent."

"I certainly hope not," I said, as my stress level elevated.

Sensing it, Sara said, "Henry Bender, you are getting tired. It is time to leave."

By now, I trusted her instincts, for she always knew the right moment to move on. Besides, these people seemed in no rush to do anything.

"Yes. Thank you for your time Father. I'll see if I can come up with something."

"Henry, watch yourself," Father warned.

"Not to worry, I will." We left.

CHAPTER 20 The Library

With so many questions still unanswered, I had to come to terms with the fact that I couldn't overturn two thousand years of history in a matter of days, much as I would've liked to.

The full scope of how much my life had been disrupted and changed was beginning to sink in. I have no intention of ending up like these people, living for a millennium like bumps on a log. One thing I knew for sure, I couldn't tolerate the way things were for much longer. I'd rather go down in flames than to continue to live like this.

However, despite all that is going on, my deep-seated desire to have a family was still there. And I couldn't figure out if it was my biology calling, a natural urge to produce offspring and create a legacy, or if it was my sex drive. Which caused me to want to live long enough to fulfill my intangible desires.

Yet, any planning for the future seemed futile, for I wasn't even sure I would survive another day. And, given these outlandish conditions, would having a healthy family even be possible? However, these were thoughts, perhaps for another time. I had to focus all my efforts on helping these people find freedom. Who in their right mind would want to bring up their kids in an environment like this? Things must be fixed.

With no viable options, a complete change had to take place. To help in that quest, I needed to get a sense of what daily life was like for the average person. I asked Sara if we could check out all the activities in those large rooms again.

She ordered, "Henry Bender, it is what we'll do tomorrow, but now you must rest."

The next morning, I was rested and ready to take on the day. My elevated positivity was a bit perplexing, not being quite sure where it was coming from.

Our second visit to the large rooms started much like the first. We entered to find people sitting on those same inflatable loungers wearing helmet-like head devices. Sara directed me to sit, and a helmet came down and covered my eyes. Instantly, it felt as if I was in another place with geometrical shapes, ranging in color and size, floating by in straight lines and circles around me. At first, I thought they were going to hit me—I ducked and dodged. Then I discovered, if I remained still, they would just travel by.

Suddenly, it occurred to me this thing might be hypnotizing me? With considerable effort, I was able to pull the helmet off my head as if it were magnetic. I was dazed; it took a moment to shake off the odd feeling of involuntarily having my head emptied.

Concerned, Sara asked, "Henry Bender, what's wrong?"

"Why, that thing was trying to brainwash me! Have you gone through this?"

"No. Father said never to do this."

"But, you let me do it!"

"You said you wanted to see how things worked."

"Oh, my… Sorry… I guess it wasn't your fault. Only, next time, tell me what not to do."

"Henry Bender, I will. Are you all right?"

"I'm okay. Now… What's next?"

"There is the relaxing room. Only this time, I will tell you, Father told me not to submit to it either."

"Thank you… However, we must check it out. Let's go."

We boarded a disk and sailed up to the next floor. So far, I hadn't seen any staircases or elevators. Again, the only way to travel up and down in the buildings was on disks. It was incredible how the thin expansive ceiling held up without more substantial structural support. As an architect, I felt it was unsound. With that many people present, I considered it to be a safety hazard. It could collapse at any moment. However, since it hadn't collapsed in hundreds of years, I had to trust it wasn't going to fall anytime soon.

The upper floor was similar to the one below. People were also reclining, but, on this level, the difference was they were listening to strange-sounding music. Its odd out of beat sound filled the room. Since Sara instructed me not to lie down, we just stood there as I examined what was going on. The people looked peaceful as if they were asleep. I could only assume it was just another way The Machine kept them mindless.

The so-called music seemed to be coming from a box, no larger than a desktop computer, sitting off to the side. Hoping it could be a way to shut The Machine down, I carefully approached it. When I came within a few feet, before I was close enough to touch it, I was struck by a massive jolt of electricity that flung me several feet back. It zapped me, and oh how it stung!

Sara screeched, "Henry Bender!"

Dazed for a moment. I quickly said," Let's get out of here before we attract any unwanted attention. Interestingly, no one seemed to notice what happened.

To me, this was another example of how The Machine maintained control. My concerns escalated, wondering if I was still under its radar? I turned to Sara, "Let's go to the Wilderness; I need to clear my head."

Upon landing, we walked along a path in silence. She then asked, "Henry Bender, are you feeling better? What do we do now?"

"Let's go see Father."

"First, you must return to a calm state. Take this time to recover from The Machine's attack before we go."

"Yes. Let's just sit right here for a while." I knew I had to unwind from the shock of almost being killed. I still felt the pain of it.

I asked her how one stays calm under these circumstances."

"I'm not sure I can explain it. What I do is to suspend my thoughts, so my chemistry signals calmness."

"What you're saying is that one must stop thinking?"

"I believe so. However, I only do it when The Machine is close enough to sense me."

"How does one know when it's sensing them?"

"It is something one learns to discern. Although there have been many who misjudged it and were treated."

"I see it's not as easy as it looks?"

"Yes, that is so. However, the Special Ones are quite perceptive."

"When did you first find out you were a Special One?"

"I have always known. I have been trained since I was a child."

"I'm glad you were." I saw her blush, for she seemed pleased with my concern.

Once I regained my composure and was calm enough, we headed out for Father's place.

On our way, I couldn't help but feel a bit nervous, as if I was on my way to be reprimanded by my old boss. Although Father was nothing like him. Yet, I saw him in a similar role—as superior to me. I feared he might lecture me for my impulsive decision to tamper with The Machine.

When we arrived, he asked, "Henry, how do you feel after your first confrontation with The Machine? You must be extra careful."

"Better, thank you," I wondered how he found out so soon.

Sara jumped in. "Henry Bender needs information."

"Henry, how can we help you?"

He made me feel comfortable, so I could focus on the task at hand. I asked, "I assume you tried everything possible to shut The Machine down?"

"Yes, of course."

"I would like to know what you've tried so far."

He explained, detailing it using technical terms, which I understood little of. I listened quietly as he rolled off a long list of attempts. I saw this was not going to be as easy as I had hoped. When finished, he said, "You see, we've tried everything we could think of. The Machine kept defeating us at every turn. It stripped away all of our capabilities. With nothing left but our wits, and fearing The Machine would treat us if we acted against it, we gave up the fight."

"Again, you conceded to live a life like this?"

"No. We decided to live in the best way we could. You're still learning how The Machine is also capable of punishment. It developed these procedures on its own and uses them on anyone who rebels against its regime. We did give up the fight, but we did so for good reasons, for exposing ourselves meant the annihilation of our spirit. It became a question of self-preservation."

"Father, with all due respect, in my day we, wouldn't have given up." I quickly checked my attitude, for I was now in their world. However, I wasn't sure if, under the same circumstances, we wouldn't have also surrendered. "I'm sorry, Father, but I'm frustrated and want to help."

"Henry, we know you do. And the only way you can do it is by doing what we cannot do. Do not be harsh on us, for much transpired in the millenniums following your times."

I asked, "What can I do you cannot do?"

"Find The Machine's vulnerabilities, and get close enough to shut it down. Those of us who still have our wits can no longer come anywhere near it without being recognized. If it detected the slightest bit of our intentions, it would treat every last one of us. However, with your invisibility and background, you are well-suited for that task."

"I see your point. But, can't you communicate with it by using those touchpads? As you did when you visited me?"

"Henry, it knows me and accepts my existence, but if it sensed rebellion in me, I would not be able to escape its treatments. Therefore, when in range of its sensors, we exercise our discipline in remaining calm, leaving us in a suspended state."

"And what is that range?"

"We judge it to be at least thirty feet of any of its components, as you learned in your shocking encounter. However, you were only given a shock due to your invisibility, but you were not treated as we would have been.

As you can see, in our unit, the ceilings are sixteen feet high, and we do not enter the empty floor below, which keeps us out of its range. Also, to protect ourselves, we secretly coated the walls and ceilings with a transparent lead-based compound we discovered in the mountains to deflect its sensors."

"Ah, that's smart. Okay, but for me to accomplish anything, I'll have to learn all I can about what could be done."

"Henry, early in my life, before The Machine existed, our past events were common knowledge. However, it was long ago, and many of those memories have faded, and all those older than me are no longer with us."

A man interrupted, "Father, is it not true there once was a place where all that information was stored?"

Another added, "Yes, I remember going there as a child long before the new city was built. I believe it was called a Library."

Others chimed in as their memories stirred.

Father added, "Yes, I did spend time there in my youth as part of my studies, but that was hundreds of years ago—by now, it may no longer exist."

"Can you take me there?"

"It was located in the old city before The Machine built the new city over it."

"Can you show me how to get there?

Another spoke up. "I believe it is still under the city."

"Under the city?" I asked, which percolated my architectural curiosity.

"Yes. That is where it would be," Father added.

"Can it be reached?"

"Henry, The Machine built our new city on piers over the old one while we were still living there. However, no one has been down there since The Machine moved us out. Consequently, we do not know if it still exists."

"Can we try to reach it?"

Henry, we can try; that is if The Machine does not occupy it. I'll choose a few who remember the most about the old city to guide you."

Another said, "I know where there's a hole that might be an entrance. I was by it some time ago and saw no sign of The Machine. I'll guide you there."

"Great. When?"

Father asked, "Is tomorrow soon enough?"

"That would be terrific!"

"Then, tomorrow, you will be taken there."

Sara ordered, "Henry Bender, you must now rest so you will be ready for tomorrow."

Heading home, my adrenaline coursed through my veins. I couldn't wait to explore this long-forgotten underground city—it was an architect's dream to do something like that.

CHAPTER 21 Retrieving The Books

Intrigued by the prospect of exploring a long-lost city. I had trouble getting to sleep. I chatted with Sara about it until she saw I was not getting the rest I needed, so she wisely had The Machine put me to sleep. After all, it did have practical uses.

Early the next morning, I said to her, "It might be better if you stayed here, it could be dangerous."

"Henry Bender, where you go, I also go." Her determination was impressive. Hence she's going wherever I go.

We met with the exploration team of four. However, it lacked Father, which I thought odd. Each carried a coil of rope on their backs. Noticeably, each had several of what they called lights, the size of one's thumb, hung on cords around their necks. Oddly, those so-called lights had no bulbs or lens looking nothing like flashlights, just solid objects.

At the cities edge, an obscure clump of vegetation covered a hole in the ground, which was believed to be an entrance. Turning on one of those lights, they dropped it in the hole. Amazingly, that one light lit the entire area below, which the guides estimated to be fifty feet deep. Courageously, one by one, we squeezed into the hole and were lowered by rope.

Once on the bottom, I was astounded at how one light lit up such a sizable area in all directions creating many forbidding shadows. Yet no blinding glare or beam was coming from the light itself; it just radiated it. It was an outstanding advancement.

So far, I hadn't seen any place where any equipment like those lights and ropes would've been kept. When I asked about it,

I was told how they hid certain items in the mountains out of the reach of The Machine. So not all resistance was dead.

In the glow, I saw a glimpse of what remained of their old city. It was crowded with numerous close-knit massive pillars. The least of which was ten feet thick and about fifty-feet-tall. All were constructed of the same gold material as the city. It was clear their close proximity was necessary to support the massive new city above.

I wondered why The Machine just didn't build it on the ground, demolishing the old city. I asked why that was so? But all they could tell me was the old city was initially built on a mound in a valley, and the new one was constructed on pillars retaining the terrain's configurations. This didn't explain the necessity for the pillars.

The guides looked to one another to reach a consensus in which direction to go. John ordered, "It is in that direction." As we pressed on, they placed the lights along our path as markers to illuminate the way. As I took in the sites, it was clear the architecture was closer to my times; being built of concrete and bricks. Noticeably, there were no buildings higher than five stories. It was surreal, almost like being on the set of one of those adventure movies I used to watch.

Hiking for a time, Sara insisted we stop and allow me to rest. I hated being weak, for I always attempted to show how strong I was. However, I was glad to stop, for I felt unsteady and didn't think I could make it much further without resting, which she seemed to instinctively know.

When rested, we resumed the trek. It took some time, trudging in the unstable soil to reach the building believed to be the library. It no longer had a roof, and the outside was engulfed with dirt piled halfway up the windows and doorways of the small single-story structure. One of the guides scurried up the accumulated dirt to the top half of a window. Attempting to open it, it crumbled in his hands. I was concerned everything inside might have also disintegrated.

Dropping a light inside the structure, causing a spooky look inside. We stood there for a moment, wondering who would go in first. As they looked at me, it left me with no choice but to drop inside, after which they followed.

The city was covered with several centuries of cobwebs and dirt, The pillars within its walls almost obliterated the space. Since the old city was covered over by the new one, it was protected from erosion by the weather. Very little had changed since the day it was abandoned, which included the dirt piles apparently caused by the pillars' placement upheaval.

It seems the pillars destroyed the possible reception and reading areas. Fortunately, remaining in the spaces between the pillars were many seemingly undisturbed small cabinets with tiny drawers. Oddly there were no books.

I looked at John, who said, "This is the Library. Let me show you."

He opened a drawer and took out a handful of what looked like thumb drives and handed me a few. They were a couple inches long and a half-inch thick and wide but lacked any sign of electronic connections or moving parts. Nor was anything written on them or on the drawers to indicate what they were.

I opened other drawers to find the contents to be the same. Okay… It made sense since paper books had become obsolete by now. Considering the volume of written history they said was there, I was amazed at how few cabinets there were.

I asked John, "Is the information we're looking for in these things?"

"Yes, everything is in these books."

It was interesting they still called them books. I asked, "How does one read them?"

He looked unsure but then said, "Ah, yes, they used players. In fact, there should be some around here."

I said, "We must find them." Searching, we found an ample supply of them in a cabinet. Each player was just large enough to cradle one book, which fit in one's clenched hand.

I asked, "How does one tell what's in them?"

He answered, "Father is more familiar with how they work. I just hope he remembers." I wondered why he hadn't come along. Perhaps, it indicated due to his age, there was a fragility in him.

Not having pockets, we used the drawers as containers. We took as many as we could safely carry, which was only a fraction of what was there.

Once back at the entrance, each of us was individually hoisted up by the ropes. I was impressed by Sara's sturdiness in hiking and being hoisted down and up. She was quite something. Once on the surface, I was glad to take a breath of fresh air; I found the old city to be claustrophobic.

Upon our return, we found Father sitting in the same spot as if he never moved. I thought maybe I should ask him about that, then decided not to.

He said, "Ah, I see you found it." We placed everything we recovered in front of him and described what we saw.

He carefully examined them and then said, "It has been so long since I last saw these. I had come to believe they no longer existed. There was a time when a person could study what they wished in these books, much as I did in my youth. The Machine took that access away when the people were relocated."

"Couldn't The Machine supply all this information to you?"

"No. It has denied allowing us to have that knowledge since it moved us out of the old city."

I couldn't help but ask, "Why couldn't you bring the books up earlier?"

"When the new city was ready, without warning, The Machine's drones quickly ushered us out of the old city, leaving us with no time to take anything with us. Afterward, many watched as the drones permanently sealed the old city, barring us from re-entry. How you got in and out is wondrous, for it was thought to be impossible."

"Father, perhaps even The Machine forgot it was there, for I believe the hole was caused by centuries of erosion."

"Ah, yes… Henry, now I must tell you things we have not spoken of for ages."

I couldn't wait to hear what he had to say as he continued, "As I explained before, in the beginning, when we programmed all the known knowledge into The Machine, some realized it was now collectively more knowledgeable than any of us.

"Even back then, some understood the advantage it had over us, which was the main reason they refused to teach it our language. Yet, no one realized the full extent of what the future would bring.

"Our leaders at the time thought we were overly-cautious. However, believing we knew better—we defied them. This was despite us being young and having no authority. Yet, the group I was working with did have control over the programming. It was our role in society, for we were the programmers. So, despite our leader's disapproval, and without their knowledge, we did what we thought was best."

"Then how come it was able to take control?"

"Henry, The Machine was the most advanced design mankind has ever conceived. Even with all our understanding, we underestimated it. On its own, and in ways still not understood by us, it started to expand its initial programming and grew in data size and function."

"You call it The Machine. Isn't there more than one?"

"No. It is one system with many appendages and separate entities; its numerous functions are controlled by one center. Much like all the functions of our body are controlled by our one brain."

"Numerous functions?"

"Ah, yes, you have not yet seen all it's capable of doing."

"I would like to see it."

"We will show you, and I believe you will be surprised. But first, I must tell you the most important thing."

Sara spoke up, "You must listen and understand what Father is about to tell you." By her tone, I wondered what could be so ominous.

He continued, "By keeping The Machine from learning our language, we denied it the ability to probe our minds. Therefore it does not hear or see what we say or do. The key to understanding our predicament is simple. However, we could not stop it from dominating every other facet of our lives. With a language of its own, it allowed it to communicate with its many parts without our involvement.

"As I explained before, there are only a few of us able to listen in on its operations, but we have no control over what it does or can know what it is planning to do. Unfortunately, by giving it a language of its own, it allowed it to become independent. Yet, despite this, it continues to follow our original programming and performs the tasks necessary to meet our needs."

"Your needs?"

"Yes, as you can see, it supplies us with food, clothing, the new city that shelters us, and the necessary treatments giving us longer lives. Leaving us with nothing left to do but to exist. I've already shared what would happen if we rebelled against it."

I could only say to him, "To be alive without a life."

"Exactly."

"Again, there was nothing you could do to control it?"

"Henry, there's a darker, a more sinister side to the story you must understand before you attempt anything."

Now that spiked my concerns. He suggested, "It is a long story; would you like something to eat before we continue?"

Exhausted and famished from our excursion to the old city, I answered, "Yes, I would. Thank you."

CHAPTER 22 A Dire Situation

I hadn't paid much attention to the floor in Father's unit even though it stood out. It was decorated with large checkerboard white and black squares in contrast to everything else being of a gold color. Each person sat on a cushion within a black square; Sara directed me to sit within one as well.

Suddenly, in front of each seated person, the white square swung open, and a small platform rose up containing a dish and a large drink container. I marveled at this, as Sara and Father noticed and smiled. However, instead of one biscuit, there were two along with an extra-large drink for each of us. It seems, even here, there was a privileged class.

As we ate, no one spoke. When finished, the tables disappeared back into the floor. It was an innovative novelty, however contrived. I was beginning to see why they had become so dependent on The Machine; it literally took care of everything—food, drink, cooking, cleaning, clothing, shelter, everything. In my day, I know many would have given anything for this.

Father said, "Henry, now for the part of the story, I believe you will find most interesting." Sara grabbed my hand as if preparing me for whatever was coming.

He continued, "In my early youth, our culture still practiced what was called family life. Although, since your times, that practice had changed considerably."

"I see it's no longer practiced at all."

"Henry, it is true. Having had two parents, I know it was built on a relationship between a man and a woman that culminated in physical bonding."

"Yes, that's what a family used to be," I responded, listening intently.

"However, it was ending about the time I was born. Being so young, I have little memory of that aspect. Added to that, so few were left able to physically practice it, caused by the debilitating physical toll humanity suffered in the war and the aftermath in the dark times.

"When my parents were young, they were among the few still capable of having that relationship but never spoke to me about it. In my early childhood, family life was no longer a viable option.

"Why?"

Because most were inflicted by a still undiagnosed malady, which made them incapable of functioning in normal procreation. However, even though I can also not perform in that capacity, I would like to know more about it. I hope you can enlighten me."

Oh my, I thought, here we go again. I had to think fast and said, "Yes, maybe at a time when we're alone." I wasn't prepared to explain that intimacy on a public platform.

"Yes, of course. Many things have evolved since your times. Mankind has always known that to survive as a species, we must reproduce our own kind. From what I understand, the use of genetic manipulation, the development of medications, and other extreme procedures eventually interfered with our natural ability to bear children. In fact, I traced that process back and found those radical changes began in your times during what was called The Sexual Revolution. Although it took ages to reach its full effect.

"No longer able to function normally, the only way left for us to multiply was by artificial means. Physical contact, once called intercourse, became obsolete."

"Are you saying it can't be done anymore?" I asked, hoping to get a positive answer."

"Henry, that is a question that remains unanswered. Once, intercourse between a man and a woman was how insemination took place. But, after The Machine was developed, some thought it was best to program it to do that job. Due to female complications caused by the extreme conditions everyone had suffered, at the time, only a few pregnancies took place, and many did not survive. It was believed The Machine could perform that job safer and with better results by using less painful protocols. At the time, we did not foresee where that decision would lead."

"You mean to say people brought this on themselves?"

"Henry, you must understand their intentions were for the good. Everything went exceedingly well at first. The Machine followed the programming to perfection. In fact, it did so well most became dependent on it, having been inflicted by that unknown malady, which still baffles us to this day, it rendered us no longer able to do it naturally.

"Although, at first, The Machine only aided in natural births. Later the parents allowed it to care for their children as well. The people were more than willing to give up that job. Under the extreme conditions, it became too stressful for them to handle it any more.

"The trouble was, The Machine lacked the human touch. In the beginning, some mothers protested and quickly took their newborns away from The Machine. However, things changed, for people had little understanding of what The Machine was capable of.

"Regrettably, because it was not seen, it was a long time before anyone realized The Machine began giving treatments to the mothers during the artificial insemination procedures without their knowledge. Treatments that made them compliant numbing their emotional connection to their offspring willingly giving their children up at birth. And even worse, it took measures to prevent most mothers from having future pregnancies.

"Most fathers were also treated simultaneously as they gave their sperm, making them impotent. People lacked understanding or even questioned what was taking place with The Machine. As unbelievable as it might seem, we now suspect the treatments were so powerful they transferred genetically to the next generation."

Hearing this sickened me, and I reacted strongly, "And they did nothing to stop it!"

"Henry, remember, by then, The Machine was developing on its own without people's input. In the beginning, its advancements were welcomed. Henry, the most dramatic change took place when The Machine figured out how to extract the necessary elements from the male and female without their knowledge or consent, which completely eliminated the natural process. A mother and father no longer were involved in the conception, carrying, birthing, and rearing of their children."

"Why would anyone want that to happen?"

"We believe it was the consequences of those treatments that left them with no will or desires of their own. At first, many thought that loss was caused by an unknown virus.

"Meanwhile, The Machine learned to repair itself and extend its capabilities to do more than anyone ever thought possible.

"Remember, no one even considered The Machine was purposely doing it, which allowed it to treat those who challenged its control without consequences. That's why it went undetected for so long."

"Again, couldn't you find some way to stop it?"

"No Henry. The process of taking over and entrenching itself took lifetimes before it reached this state. As The Machine continued to prolong our lives and meet all of our needs, we became complacent and easily gave in."

"You mean, you willingly gave up your freedom."

"In a way, I suppose we did, but not as willing as you might think. As I said earlier, when we were still able to modify its programs, a few saw the direction it was headed."

"At that point, couldn't you still shut it down?"

"Perhaps, however, in the beginning, when The Machine was benefitting us, they made it indestructible; it was believed this would keep it from being tampered with by unauthorized people. Consequently, we became weaker as The Machine grew stronger."

"And you didn't resist?"

"Before you judge us, let me tell you all that took place."

In my reaction, I realized I was being disrespectful and said, "Sorry, Father, it's frustrating to see what has happened to my world."

"Henry, we understand your feelings, and now you must also understand as much as we do, for you might be the last chance to save humanity."

"Me! Save humanity—the last chance? How can one person
do that?" When I said that, they all smiled as if they knew something I didn't.

Father said, "Henry, please trust us."

I saw they either had no answers or didn't yet want to reveal them to me. These people's way of thinking was still a mystery to me. Even Sara mystified me at times. However, I realized I was now in their world and didn't feel I should keep accusing them or had any power to do anything.

Father continued, "Eventually, we discovered by creating The Machine, we placed ourselves in a dire situation."

"Dire?"

"Yes Henry. The Machine took away our ability to reproduce and neutered all those who openly defied it. Unfortunately, we still know almost nothing about combating those treatments or what they comprise, leaving us defenseless. The Machine treated almost everyone. Fearing discovery by its sensors, those of us who still possessed a mind of our own were forced to hide. Had we not, there would be no human spirit left— perhaps no humans at all."

"Henry, our resources in fighting it are exhausted. We have done our best to remain undetected, hoping to be saved, but our time is now running out."

"But, doesn't The Machine have a symbiotic relationship with you? It must have some idea of what you're thinking. It still takes care of you, doesn't it?"

"Henry, it is complicated. In adjusting its programs, we had some success. As I said, we were able to blind it to understand what we did. Unfortunately, its sensors could detect when we were experiencing stress, dissatisfaction, or rebellion, by monitoring our chemistry changes. When it discovers any disharmony, it administers those treatments."

"Is that what you meant by dire?"

"It is only part of it. Let me tell you more."

It was dire enough for me. I couldn't imagine anything being worse.

"Henry, as I described, physical intercourse is no longer applicable. People are no longer involved in that process other than a few men and women supplying the two essential ingredients that create life—The semen and the egg.

"Forgive me for asking, since you are called Father, does that mean you are the supplier of those ingredients?"

"Not exactly, Henry. I am one of the few left to supply sperm, although no longer to naturally do it by physical contact. The Machine abstracts it from me only when needed. What is extraordinary is that I am unaware of when it takes place. But there will come a time none of us will be left to supply the ingredients. Something must be done, and soon."

Talk about being dire. This was it. Apparently, Father was one of the few passing on our genetic code. Was this not a form of inbreeding, with him perhaps fertilizing his daughters' eggs, so to speak? However, I saw it was not a good time to bring that up.

Without pause, Father continued, "Since we initially programmed it to take care of us, it still routinely performs that task, even though it appeared to have no interest in relating to us. "After all this time, it continues to do so. And as it further develops, we believe someday soon it will eliminate all of our original programs and replace it with its own."

"Does that mean it will no longer take care of you?"

"Yes, we believe so. We think it is learning that it is just as enslaved to us as we are to it. We see signs in its behavior that indicates it is moving slowly in that direction—seeking its freedom from us. If that happens, the human race will not survive."

"Wow. So, you're asking me to save humanity? Look, I'm no superhero. But, on the other hand, I must say I do like a challenge! What can I do to help?"

"Henry, even though it nursed, fed, and clothed you, we believe its sensors does not recognize you. It does not pick up your distress as if you do not exist. Meaning it cannot detect your state-of-mind.

"Remember when you got too close to it? Although you received quite a jolt, it did not try to control you. The shock you received was because you entered its zone—not because it picked up your chemical singles. Otherwise, it would have treated you. This leads us to believe you can do things we cannot. That is if you are willing?"

"Of course I'm willing. I'll do whatever is necessary. It seems I have no choice, do I?"

"For the sake of us all, I'm afraid not. However, we hope you can help before it's too late."

"What do you mean, too late?"

"This is what we fear. In the beginning, it was believed it would help accomplish the universal goal of people never needing to labor again. The Machine was to supply everything required for our survival. All that would remain for us to do was to be alive.

"We were to live an idyllic life, but, as you see, it did not turn out well for us. The Machine further developed its power, and not by our direction. It built a complex system to do all things necessary for our survival. However, while constructing its system, it did not consider our input or even our best interests."

"I can see how not having to labor was appealing. But isn't life about working and making your own decisions?"

"Henry, in my youth, people still labored, but not many. You see, by then, most had already become dependent. Again, as I said, a number of significant turning points took place in your times. However, those who were successful in accumulating power became dictators.

Back then, some concluded the system was an unequal one. They felt all should be equal. It was mistakenly thought, if one had no more than another, it would solve the inherent problems we all face."

I said, "Yes, in my times, many people latched onto the idea of not having to work for their share."

"Henry, instead of finding a utopia, it led to the Great War, which nearly annihilated humanity. People are not equal. Each person is unique with differing abilities. Unfortunately, there are those who seek power over others and those who willingly submit to them. And there are some who are able to resist corruption and seek independence and freedom. However, the worst offenders are those who do not want to get involved in the struggle to keep their human rights.

"Once upon a time, people understood that to maintain a sound social structure, a fair and just balance was necessary. However, those old ways were abandoned."

"I'm afraid I'm beginning to see that."

"That is good, Henry. After the devastation of the war, it took lifetimes of dormancy before humanity began to dig out of the hole it had dug. However, even after all the world had been through, people had not learned the past lessons.

"Therefore, instead of making the corrections needed, people set out on the same path by building a computer to eliminate the need to work or even to think for themselves."

"The old panacea, right?"

"Yes… I'm afraid mankind has always sought that. At the time, in theory, The Machine seemed to be an excellent idea. However, we could not have been more wrong. We have come to understand that our lack of participation and inactivity has led to the most drastic consequence—bringing mankind towards its end."

"What end?"

"Sorry, Henry, we want you to fully appreciate what you must do to help."

"If I can help, I will. But I don't understand. What can I do that you cannot?"

"As I said, you are invisible to The Machine. All of us are under its surveillance and cannot act in the slightest way against it. Consequently, we practice a strict devotion to calmness. This dedication leaves us unable to take action."

"I see… What are you asking of me?"

"We believe we failed by not giving The Machine the ability to have feelings or, at the very least, a sympathetic understanding of us. As you might say, it lacks compassion. We programmed it to take care of us, not to care about us. Although, we now believe the latter might have been an impossible task.

"Up to this point, it has only affected our minds, which is devastating in itself. However, lately, as I said, we believe it is coming to the conclusion that it no longer has a reason to sustain us."

"Are you saying it is going to exterminate you?"

"No, it will merely stop taking care of us, and in the state of mind most of us are in, we will not be able to care for ourselves. This is the catastrophic result of putting technology before our humanness."

"What you are saying is mankind has lost its purpose."

"Yes, we believe that is the situation we now find ourselves in."

"I think I understand. But what do you want me to do?"

"Henry, we must shut it down, and we believe you are the Chosen One to do it."

"Wow! Wait a minute. If we shut it down, won't there be consequences?"

"Absolutely, and likely our lives will be shortened. We will have to take care of ourselves and, more importantly, learn how to labor. Many of us will not survive."

"Are you willing to do that?"

"It is better than having no life at all. If the treated ones are no longer able to care for themselves, it would be up to us, the few in this room, to maintain order and tend to what's left of humankind. Without the participation of all, it is a task we cannot fulfill."

"I see your point."

Father concluded. "Good. I think we have done enough for today,"

"Henry Bender, you must have nutrition and rest," Sara ordered.

I was hungry and stressed out beyond anything I'd ever experienced. Who wouldn't be after hearing all this? Was I strong enough to accomplish what they were asking of me? However, I saw no alternative—it was The Machine or us.

CHAPTER 23 The Supply Chain

It wasn't until I returned to my unit that I realized how uptight I was. I needed to unwind. Although I was regaining confidence, strength, and more weight each day. I was was still weak, and my body was a skeleton of my former physique. Feeling a little depressed, I said to Sara, "I'm not sure I can do what's being asked of me."

"Henry Bender, of course you can. You are the Chosen One."

"Is that what you really think?"

"Henry Bender. Yes, it is. Why else would you be here?"

I smiled, loving her simplicity, not yet buying it. Still, there was little sense in trying to convince her otherwise. Anyway, it made me feel good when she said those things, giving me the incentive I needed.

She ordered, "Now, Henry Bender, please lie down and rest. You must be ready for tomorrow."

"Okay, I will." Exhausted, I didn't even need The Machine to help me fall asleep.

I awoke the next morning after a long deep sleep, rested and better motivated. It was time to charge on. First, I needed a plan, for I'd painfully learned I couldn't rush an attack on The Machine.

I asked Sara if she had any suggestions, realizing I hadn't given her enough credit as a valuable resource.

She answered, "I think you should see more of what The Machine does."

"Okay, show me."

Before long, we were flying in the clouds thousands of feet high, over the mountains. The impenetrable mountains totally blocked off the city from the rest of the island. On the windward side, there were cultivated fields that stretched into the distance. The island was much larger than I had expected, for it extended over the horizon.

Observing from flying high up on a disc, I saw an assortment of crops—looking like wheat, corn, vegetables, and others I couldn't identify, being a city boy. They were all growing in abundance. There were even orchards.

I asked, "Can we go in closer?"

"Henry Bender, I've been here many times; I have always been afraid to go any closer, for I do not know what might happen."

"I see parts to examine for any weaknesses."

"Then that is what we will do," she boldly replied.

We descended to just above the plants, where I felt the fear of being discovered. However, when seeing her peaceful expression, I thought this woman was braver than anyone I knew. How could I cower and let her down?

The Machine parts were doing the work of many farmers. Odd-looking driverless wheeled vehicles of various types plowed some sections, cultivated others, and harvested the ready crops.

I asked, "Has anyone ever tried to approach any part of The Machine out here?"

"From what I understand, those who touched or came too close received the same punishment you received, and not to their liking, they were treated. It is said, some even lost their lives." That was not encouraging, but it was interesting to be so close to the operation despite that fear. The Machine parts didn't react to us; it was as if we were invisible. Apparently, we weren't considered a threat, which was a blessing. I understood why I was invisible, but Sara did not have the same advantage, yet she maintained the calm persona called for. I looked at her strength with adoration.

After observing as much as I could take in, I said, "Okay, what's next?"

She took me to an open area where The Machine parts were delivering the harvest. There were no buildings with roofs to protect the massive processing operation, as there would be if humans were in charge. Specialized parts did all the cleaning, sorting, cutting, and cooking of the produce.

As we hovered over it, it was fascinating to watch how quickly they transformed the wide variety of crops into those biscuits and drinks, which was the only type of food product it produced. There were vats of different batches of ingredients being mixed to be compressed into those biscuits.

Despite creating a variety of incredible tastes in the biscuits, it seemed dull not to experience the tangible differences in the chewing of different types of foods. Not that The Machine cared about such things. However, the task was to look for any weak spots, not knowing what they might be. I just took in everything I saw.

"Okay, what's next?"

She took me further out to an area filled with manufacturing-type machinery, also out in the open without shelter. The tightly packed equipment was operating at full blast, leaving no room for a person to pass through. She explained that all the necessary supplies were made there. I saw serving trays, drink containers, clothing, cushions, beds, chairs, tables, and even flying disks—everything. It was still hard to believe that each piece of equipment was actually part of one Machine.

I could only imagine how extensive and complicated the system had to be to get everything to where it had to be without any human input. The greater mystery was how did The Machine know where things were supposed to go? Not having a clear answer to that question, she further explained how most people had no idea this complex system existed.

Since there was no passage for people through or around the mountains, The Machine designed and built the delivery labyrinth underground. It was the only way to continually move the massive amount of goods other than by disks, which was labor-intensive. I was astonished when she told me how little people cared to know about this intricate system. She explained everything quite well.

I looked at her and could onlywondered who she could be? Impressed with her knowledge of the operation, I could only think she had to be someone extra special.

Interestingly, it occurred to me, why hadn't The Machine cleared a path through the mountains for people to travel through, which I believed it was capable of doing. Sara had no answer. I could only conclude; it didn't consider that access was necessary, or perhaps it was a matter of control over the people. Both ways, it was troubling. Which made it more critical for the people to gain back control of the things that served them. The Machine had too much power over them. I wished I could go back to my day and somehow tell the people they were on the wrong technological path. But then again, who would've listened?

In hindsight, it's easy to see how, in my day, we plunged ahead in the name of progress, without thinking about where it would lead. It was now evident that the industrial and technological revolutions' results didn't turn out as beneficial in the long run as was once believed. It was disheartening.

Sara sensed my concern, "Henry Bender, what is troubling you?"

"Sara, am I really, the only hope?"

"Yes, Henry Bender, you are."

I sighed, feeling the pressure of it all. How was I to save the human race? Then, it occurred to me; there might be helpful information in the materials we took from the library. I said to her, "We need to see Father."

Once there, I said to Father, "If I could read what was taken from the library, I might be able to figure out how to shut The Machine down."

"Henry, we no longer read," Father said. "In fact, written language has been obsolete for more than fifteen hundred years. As you see, all knowledge was recorded visually and orally in these books until the day it was all taken away."

I wasn't surprised, for I remember even back in my day, they were predicting paper books would become obsolete. Since technology advanced at such a rapid rate in my times, it made sense that almost nothing would be the same. Although, given the deplorable conditions of these people, any advancements came at a high cost. I picked up one of the books and asked, "How do I turn it on? Are the batteries still good?"

He smiled and said, "That is old technology." Our power sources are much more advanced. Let me show you." He inserted a book into a player, and, to my amazement, a colorful life-sized, three-dimensional hologram of a man appeared and began to speak. Seeing my wonder, he pulled the book out of the player, shutting it off, and said, "You see, we have been quite industrious since your times."

"Fascinated, I asked, "Now, how will I find the information I'm looking for?"

Father said to the pile of books, "How did the Great War start?" and a few books glowed. "You see, Henry, it is that easy."

I asked, "Father, how long will its power last?"

"Henry, do not be concerned, for in the past, none of the books have ever run out of power, and I suspect they will not in one lifetime."

Again, I couldn't help but be astounded, although I was getting used to that feeling. I asked, "Father, can I take the books with me?"

"Henry, take whatever you need. But there's a better way. John will prepare it for you. Time is of the essence."

Rather than asking again what he meant about the time, I opted to first study the books, for I still felt there were things Father might not be telling me.

John spread out the books on the floor and passed a player over them. It was still hard to think of them as books. As he did, one by one, they glowed, and, just as quickly as they lit up, they dimmed. When done, he handed me the player and said, "All that was brought back is now in here. Just ask what you seek, and it will tell you."

As unbelievable as it was, I smiled, took it, and said to Sara,

"Let's go."

She asked, "Henry Bender, where do we go now?"

"I would like to go to the Wilderness."

"Then that is where we will go."

CHAPTER 24 The Books

We landed in the Wilderness out of sight of others under a tree in the heavily wooded area. I held the player up and spoke to it, "The Great War?" and, as if by magic, a life-sized hologram appeared. There were no electronic light beams or connection between him and the player. It was as if he was flesh and blood standing by us. I must admit it was exciting to see, for he seemed so real, although hazy. He was dressed in an unfamiliar clothing style, nothing like the people here were wearing or from my times, having more flair.

However, the image just stood there. I looked at Sara, not knowing what to do. She said, "Maybe you should say something to him?"

I asked, "Sir, will you tell me how the Great War started?" and, to my delight, he began to speak. But, rather than looking at us, he peered into space. It was as if we were watching a video of him giving a lecture. He was totally unaware of us.

He said, "After a long period of peace when our landmass was still connected, people were becoming more divided than ever. Instead of bringing them together, The Age of Information only highlighted their differences, which caused significant friction among the opposing factions."

Disputes erupted over territory, belief systems, philosophies, and economics. The corrupt who sought power took advantage of the chaos. The information outlets, which once were relatively unbiased, had become one-sided in either direction. They were filled with misinformation to satisfy one group or another.

Secular and even religious powers fell into the hands of

fewer and fewer leaders who seemed more interested in retaining control than informing.

"Consequently, for one to survive, they were forced to pick a group to side with, which was necessary for one to gain protection. There was no longer a middle ground for one to stand.

"However, despite all this, in this period, catastrophic worldwide wars were averted. But this changed when a new leader emerged, called "The One." He campaigned in the name of peace and love winning the hearts of many. Yet, when he gained absolute power, he twisted his hopeful campaign into an evil regime. At the peak of his power, he ordered his followers to eliminate all opposing factions causing blood to flow in the streets. It was a sight no one would ever want to see.

"As the annihilation began, something mysterious took place. Within one day, the skies became so bright people had to cover their eyes. All viewing screens around the world cut to the same blinding glow. People interpreted what was happening in different ways to suit their beliefs.

"With the multiple interpretations, it only confused the people leaving them at a loss in what actually took place on that one particular day, as twenty percent of the world's population vanished and was never seen again—not even their remains. Because of this, many believed the world was ending.

"Despite that horrific catastrophe, The One ordered the killing to continue in an attempt to exterminate all remaining resistance.

Eventually, it forced those who once revered him to rebel in fear he would abolish them too. The more he killed, the more people turned against him. Those who survived eventually slew him, along with his most ardent followers, ending the war.

"However, by that point, the human race was decimated. It took lifetimes before the spirit of man would reawaken. When it did, people began to rise up again. Unfortunately, they had to rebuild from the ground up.

"They vowed never again to go to war. Yet, it still took many decades to rediscover and begin the work of establishing a connected society. Fortunately, one day they unearthed the recorded knowledge from the past, which they thought in the years of conflict was lost forever.

This gave them hope.

The hologram disappeared, and I concluded, "I guess that's all he had to say," which was more than I could absorb at the moment.

I compared Father's recollection to what the hologram said—they were close but not exactly the same. I wondered who this speaker was and what gave him the authority to speak of such matters? He recounted the facts as if he were a third party, seemly having full knowledge of what had taken place.

Sara said, "It must have been awful for those people."

"Sara, no more so than what has happened to your people."

"Henry Bender, do you really think so?"

"I do. And, if we don't find a solution fast, I fear what Father said about the human race ending will come true."

"Oh, my."

I said, "Let's watch another one," and asked the player, "What happened next?" To my glee, another hologram rose up. However, this time a different person appeared, dressed in another clothing style. I couldn't describe his dress either, other than it being futuristic looking. I wondered if that indicated the passage of time or if people simply wore what they pleased.

He spoke. "When the war was over, the known population had diminished to only a fraction of what it once was. Miraculously, despite the devastation, a storehouse of information survived. However, during the extended period of darkness that followed the war, that information lay dormant while humankind existed only a step above animals.

"After the lost knowledge was finally rediscovered, it took some time before people understood the importance of it.

Once that was realized, the smartest among them worked hard to restore the Age of Information. Still, it took an incredible span of time for them to figure out how to interpret and make use of it.

"By then, there were no living survivors of the war. However, their descendants began to reestablish new institutions of learning based on that pre-war knowledge. They hoped to build a society whose only purpose was to serve the people rather than living under cruel dictatorial powers.

"Meanwhile, in the natural course of cosmic evolution, the world warmed. The rising waters accelerated, causing many to fear a flood would consume all the landmass. Fortunately, before that occurred, the rising waters stabilized.

"Once the people felt secure enough, they wanted to get on with life. The wisest decided to build one computerized system that was capable of fulfilling all the people's needs. At the time, it seemed to be an inspired idea. Despite its shortcomings, after all the misery inflicted on mankind, they wanted to create a life of peace and safety. So, in that effort, they embarked on building a perfect machine that would meet mankind's every need." He finished speaking and disappeared.

Each book had a slightly different take on past history. So absorbed in the stories, we didn't even think of eating.

We opened another one, and a new image rose up. This time, it was a woman wearing a different clothing style from the others, which I couldn't reference to any period I knew of. She was proof that in earlier times, people still had the freedom to choose what they wore. I asked her, "What happened next?"

Also speaking into space, with no awareness of us, she said, "As the development of The Machine began, people relaxed into the assurance that this was the answer to finding peace and safety. As time went on, society entrusted more and more of its self-care to The Machine. As a result, people were left with little to do. Many became lethargic and just sat around, waiting to be served. Yet, the most disturbing development was to come.

"In time, The Machine had developed beyond its original programming. It was taking control as people slowly relinquished their power to it. A few tried to modify or even reverse its programming.

However, The Machine had become too powerful. Some hoped to someday be set free, and had to remain hidden for their survival." With that said, the image withdrew, leaving us to wonder what she meant?

We sat still for a moment, attempting to sort it out.

Father mentioned all this, but to hear it from the people who lived it, was really powerful. I was intrigued by how they shared these events. Although, they spoke more as historians rather than participants. It was clear those people were smart and should've known better.

Sara hadn't heard this history and was as moved as I was. She asked, "Henry Bender, what is there to be done?"

"I think we'd better have something to eat. I need time to think."

"Yes, Henry Bender."

CHAPTER 25 Called To The Beach

Back in my unit, Sara asked many questions—much as a child would. I saw an enthusiasm emerging in her, which motivated me even more so to take action. I wanted to see her happy and free from this cruel existence.

These people seem to believe I was the one to set them free, but how? I was still weak; yet, on the other hand, I also knew The Machine was only a machine and was initially programmed by men. Many thoughts raced through my head as I pieced together the history lessons I had just taken in.

"Henry Bender, what is next?" she asked, almost as if she knew she had to get me focused. Seeing how she looked at me, I realized I had to shake any fears and doubts. Just as I did when I challenged myself to those daredevil feats. Maybe, the discipline I developed in doing all my stupid stunts was in preparation for this?

I answered her, "Look, as I keep saying, all machines have flaws. All we have to do is to find one weakness that will allow us to shut it off."

A thought struck me, and I asked her, "Can The Machine pick up the playing of the books. She assured me we were out of range of its probing, which was a relief. With that, I asked the player, "What happened next?"

A hologram emerged, this time of a man, who said, "The Machine began developing beyond human understanding. It treated people's physical ills, fed and clothed them, and prolonged their lives as they programmed it to do. However, as it carried out those functions, it also began to develop further on its own. As time passed, it assumed more and more control over the people's movements and behavior.

"Only a small number recognized the possible dangers. They tried to reprogram it with little success. In desperation, they even attempted to shut it down. But their efforts were unsuccessful.

"In time, they reluctantly came to accept it had a mind of its own. To their horror, it developed treatments to punish those who contested or rebelled against its operation.

"Fortunately, there were a few who discover how to remain unnoticed by it. Because of the reprogramming efforts, The Machine was unable to see or hear the people. However, it was still able to pick up chemical changes caused by an individual's stress level.

"Consequently, when in close proximity to The Machine, people had to remain calm. However, given the trying circumstances, this was an unnatural state to maintain. In time, most were unable to control their feelings or behavior and were treated. Those who successfully avoided the treatments could only wonder how long these unacceptable conditions would last.

"When The Machine finished erecting the new city over the old one, it took away all the people's capabilities to regain control. Everyone was herded out of the ancient city by drones using electrified probes to forcibly move them into the new city. No one was allowed to take anything with them. If one tried, they received a jolt causing them to drop what they were carrying. The Machine became invincible, leaving the people in bondage until someone would come to shut it down.

"This may be the last recording, for it's taking away all our means of electronic communications." The image withdrew. Once again, we were stunned. Wanting to know more, I asked, "What happened next?" There was no response. Apparently, it was actually the last communication before The Machine seized complete control. All recorded human history had ceased.

Sara asked, "Is my world so terrible?"

"I'm afraid so. These books keep repeating the same story

from different views. It looks like The Machine is on a path to eliminate us. We must shut it down."

"Henry Bender, I believe you are the one to do it. You can do anything. Remember, you are the Chosen One. Even Father sees that."

I loved her for saying that, but I still wasn't sure how to pull it off. At a loss, I could only think to say, "Sara, we must study The Machine and these books from as many angles as possible. Hopefully, to find whatever we might've missed."

"Yes, Henry Bender. However, it is getting late; you need to rest. Tomorrow, we will study more."

"Okay, I'll rest for now." I still couldn't figure out how much sensitivity she had in this dumb-downed world to know when I was exhausted. Her caring overwhelmed me—even in my world, most people weren't that perceptive.

The next morning, I awoke with a renewed hope of fixing this place. From what the books indicated, I wondered if they understood what was going on when recorded. If so, why did they allow it to continue? On the other hand, I felt I was beginning to figure out what was missing, which involved much the same issues that were taking place in my day. I saw how the hopes of solving problems to make a better world might have been based on some faulty premises.

I was beginning to realize how much thought and energy it takes to make the world better. Maybe solving all problems has always been and will remain an impossible dream. Yet, paradoxically, I believe humankind has always sought purposeful solutions. It seems that's what humans do better than any other creature. Apparently, most people had lost the ability to find purpose causing them to become mindless zombies.

It apparently took decades for each new round of corrupted thinking to emerge, undermining the social structure leading many down dead-end paths. Was it going to be up to me alone to figure out what could be done?

Suddenly, out of nowhere, it struck me, as I remembered from my Sunday School teachings; I figured out Armageddon took place at the beginning of the Great War? If so, most likely, these people are the descendants of those whom God rejected and left behind.

It was a chilling thought, and I didn't know where it came from. But it suddenly made sense in why all those people disappeared in just one day, and those still here appear to be condemned to live in this hell-like existence. It is like what was predicted in the book of Revelation.

I kind of knew what that book predicted concerning the end times from my childhood days of going to church. If those teachings were true, had the world I knew ended? If so, why are these people still here? If this is hell, is there a way out? Would it take another Adam and Eve situation for humanity to be reborn? Something for sure died in these people. And at this point, I could only speculate on what it was and if there's any hope left.

Suddenly, Sara said, "We must go. The Machine parts are gathering on the beach."

"How do you know that?"

"I just know."

I trusted her, for I understood there were still things I knew little about. I felt a little faint and had to use the staff to help myself onto the disk. Although I didn't want Sara to view me as an invalid, I loved seeing her concern for me. Maybe, deep down, I was still just a little kid who craved loving attention. Although there was no justification for such thoughts.

I was beginning to see my life through different eyes. I did those dumb stunts to feel good about myself. Even with the love of Cecilia, I was too cowardly to step out on my own and accomplish something good and great. Why did I spend so much time wallowing? Why did I choose to focus on what was missing instead of what I had?

Oh, how small a life I led! Yes, I made good money, but what did it matter when it left me frustrated and unfulfilled? Nevertheless, I now find myself immersed in important issues, and I didn't want to screw it up this time.

We landed on top of the cliffs where Roger and the children were waiting. Peering down from the edge, I saw Machine parts of all sizes and shapes crowded together on the beach. Curious and not knowing what to make of it, I ordered, "Let's just watch and see what we can see."

Parts were still arriving from all directions. Hovering as one by one, they landed and shut down. At that point, we could only watch and wait.

Rodger said, "In the past, when all arrived, they would go to sleep for at least a day. Then, while we slept during the night, they would disappear."

"I take it you never went any closer?" I asked.

Sara said, "Henry Bender, as children, we were told to never go near or touch The Machine unless it invites us to do so."

"Sara, I could only think this is The Machine's way of either giving or receiving something, albeit it's only a guess. I hope whatever is going to take place will reveal The Machine's weaknesses. Roger, even when the parts were asleep, you didn't go any closer?"

"No, of course not. We kept away out of fear."

"Henry Bender, what do we do now?"

"Sara, we can only watch to see what it's up to."

As we waited, The Machine parts continued to land.

Meanwhile, the children brought us lunch. I figured it would take at least the rest of the day for all the parts to arrive from what they told me. Deciding to make our stay as comfortable as possible, the children piled their bed pads on large disks, which they called in at will, and flew them to the cliff's edge. We all settled down to watch the incredible sight.

The different parts had various configurations, which indicated each had a particular function. I asked the children if they knew what any of those were. They described what they had seen a number of them do. Most were mundane tasks, and others I couldn't figure out.

It was apparent how alive and active the children were as they watched everything around them and to describe it in detail. I had to keep that spirit of theirs alive, for it gave me the incentive to take action. Since I knew it would take a while, we took turns watching so as not to exhaust anyone. I spent some time listening to the children as they described what they had seen in the past.

I used their descriptions to piece together how The Machine was able to maintain control. I saw how it created a complex operation with many safeguards to protect itself from disruption. It was exhausting to sort things out, and I soon decided to get some rest.

Later, Sara woke me and ordered, "Henry Bender, you need to eat." She always knew when it was best to say that. I ate, and then, still tired, I took another respite. I made sure everyone knew their job and then ordered them to wake me if anything changed. Making myself comfortable, I said to Sara, "Come, you must rest too."

"Yes, Henry Bender."

It was not long before both of us were asleep, putting our trust in the children.

CHAPTER 26 The Big Charge

The next morning, as the sun began to rise, Roger woke me and said, "Come see."

I called Sara, waking her. Looking out from the cliffs, to see many parts below. All were now shut down. However, this time, hefty metallic tentacles connect each component to the one next to it. It formed what I thought to be a simple circuit. Although it seemed too simplistic for such advanced technology.

I needed time to think about this new finding. I turned to Sara, clenched her hand, and we flew back to the deserted children's compound. A place where I could think better with just the two of us.

Seeing the intensity of my thoughts, she asked, "Henry Bender, what are you thinking?

"I suspect we're about to see something unusual."

"Then we must get back and watch," she said, stating the obvious.

"I'm afraid so. But I need to relax for a few minutes."

In a short while, after having breakfast and being more relaxed and calmer, we returned to the cliff's edge to be with the children. Nothing new had occurred. Remarkably, The Machine obviously still had no idea of what we were up to. It seemed not to be as smart as they credited it with.

With all the parts now connected, I expected something extraordinary to happen. From the children's prior observations, it could be another day before anything occurred. Till then, all we could do was to take turns watching.

There were no signs of activity for the rest of the day.

Meanwhile, the children spent their free time playing rough-and-tumble games with a high degree of energy. Watching them reminded me of the children in my day, which made me smile. As the day went on, and the sun sank into darkness, our watch continued. Most went to sleep, including Sara and I, leaving just a few to watch.

Then… in the middle of the night suddenly, a rumbling in the ground awoke everyone. Panic set in, and the children gathered around me. I ordered, "Keep your eyes on the beach." In the moonlight, we were only able to see the silhouettes of the parts. Nothing seemed amiss. As the rumbling increased, our fear and dismay grew. We had no idea what was going on. Offshore, the waters began to stir. I yelled to Roger, "Do you know what this is?"

"We have never been out here at night, although we have felt this rumbling before."

Sara asked, "Henry Bender, what do we do now?"

"We watch. We watch," was all I could say.

Mystified, our eyes focused on the waters as its turbulence grew to a volatile level. Then, a brightly lit massive object rose up from the depths and hovered above the water, illuminating the entire area.

It was an enormous block that I estimated to be at least a hundred feet square. Suddenly it sent out an explosive lightning charge traveling through the air. The jolt touched only one part, which sent a shockwave through all of the interlinked parts. The charge then streaked off toward the city.

Energized, the parts came to life, rising up and flying off in mass, disappearing into the dark skies. Then the block went dark and returned to the depths of the ocean, and the waters became calm as if nothing had occurred.

Dumbfounded, we just sat there for a long moment. Then Roger asked, "What was all that?"

"I believe we found its source of power."

Immediately, and not to my liking, the children impulsively ran down to the beach, frantically looking around. I was relieved and thankful their impulsive move didn't put them in harm's way. After a while, with nothing more to see, Sara asked, "Henry Bender, what do we do now?"

"I think we go home, get some rest, and return tomorrow. A good night's sleep and a new day will give us a fresh perspective."

"Then let us go." She turned to the children and ordered, "You are all safe now. Go back to your area and get some sleep. We will see you tomorrow."

CHAPTER 27 The Examination

The next morning I again experienced the same old uncertainties. Would I make it? Was I smart enough? However, in my world, it only involved me. This time, my actions would affect everyone, and I wondered if I was made of the right stuff to carry it through. If this was a dream, it definitely felt like an impossible dream that mankind hasn't solved.

I couldn't help but share my doubts with Sara. She said, in her simple way, "Henry Bender, who else is there to save us but you?"

Whether she understood it or not, her statement made the point and gave me the impetus I needed to start the day. However, I couldn't forget my stupidity in my former life. No doubt, I deeply affected and damaged Cecilia's entire life. That thought was so unbelievably painful, it remains to be something I'll never recover from.

But now, I feared the possible loss of another life—a life with Sara and this entire world of lost souls. The results of this failure would be catastrophic—it was not an option. I could only question, is this really happening to me? However, when Sara looked at me, her steadiness gave me the strength to hold the rudder on course.

After breakfast, I was more confident as we boarded a disk and flew to the cliffs. The children were still camped out, for they had not obeyed Sara's orders to return to the compound. However, I regarded their behavior as a good sign, for they were only acting as kids naturally do—curious and a bit mischievous. They gathered around, wanting to know what was next. I boldly led them down to the water's edge to where the block had submerged.

After a moment of silence, Roger asked, "What do we do now?"

"I hate to say this, but I believe we need to check and see if the block is out there," which was the only move I could think of.

A child asked, "Is it alright with The Machine to do that?"

I saw how much work it was going to take to get their minds straight. However, I said, "Don't worry. I'll fly out first and take a look, for it could be dangerous."

"We must go with you!" Roger said.

"It's too dangerous."

"You are willing to put your life in danger for our sake. We must also be prepared to do so for our own sake, is that not so?"

"Henry Bender, Roger has a point," Sara said.

I thought for a moment. Rationalizing, since these children had the most to lose, it seemed only right to let them help. Yet, I was reluctant to expose them to any danger. In my world, I would've said, absolutely not." But this is their world, and if it could be saved, it would not only be for me but more so for them to do. Which meant they had to learn and be willing to take chances, however dangerous.

Still conflicted, with much concern, I ordered, "Okay… Then let's do it. But remember, no matter the circumstances, don't touch the block."

I had no idea if anything disastrous would happen. In fact, I was scared to death, not so much for myself but for their safety. Nevertheless, and contrary to common sense, I decided I couldn't deny them having their part.

In hovering on disks over the spot where the block went down, it was easy to spot it in the clear water not far below the surface. The thought of entering the water was scary, but I felt determined to examine it up close. I ordered, "I'll go in first to test it. Now don't jump in until I signal you. And remember, don't go off on your own; we must stay together. And again, don't touch it." I was still questioning how wise this was, but I couldn't back out now. I dove in and plunged toward the object. After taking a quick look, without anything terrible happening, I surfaced.

From that moment on, their safety became my number one priority. This was the first time I'd ever put another's life in danger. I felt the weight of that responsibility. Whether I liked it or not, this was war, and in war, dangerous things do occur.

On disks, I ordered them to surround the perimeter to find each corner. When everyone was in place, I motioned for all to jump in. The water had to be at least a hundred feet deep to cover the block. We found its surface was smooth with rounded edges. Its gold color was highly polished, and there were no openings, indentations, or protrusions. Since it was impossible to dive down to its full depth, I limited the search to only examining its top.

Out of breath, I surfaced and waved everyone back to the beach, but again they already knew to do so. Since it was hard to mount the disks from the water, we swam back as the empty disks followed us to the beach. I couldn't figure out, since The Machine wasn't able to understand our language, how did the disks know what we wanted them to do? Again, no one had satisfying answers.

I was amazed at how well the children swam and could only think how much potential these children had that would be lost if we failed in freeing them. I thought they must have swum a lot at the beach. I wondered why they never spotted the block before. Perhaps it was too far offshore or, more likely, since it had always been there, it was not considered to be something unusual.

Reaching the shore, I laid down on the beach to catch my breath. I thought I was a strong swimmer but found the children had me beat; they were in good shape. We rested for a few minutes, and then I asked, "Did anyone see anything unusual about the block?"

Several children spoke, but the only thing anyone could comment on was how smooth it was. I wonder if it was solid or if there was something inside it.

I looked at Sara, who shrugged her shoulders. I said, "Tomorrow, we'll go see Father," hoping he had some knowledge of what it was. Curious and unsure if there would be another incident, we spent the rest of the day with the children for their safety.

As darkness fell, feeling confident, nothing more was going to happen. Deciding to leave, Sara instructed the children to keep watching, reminding them to stay off the beach and out of the water.

CHAPTER 28 Studying The Block

Arriving back in my unit, I walked through the ring to refresh myself. I was impressed with its performance. It even removed the sand, sucking it into a hole at the base of the ring.

I asked Sara what she thought of what we saw.

"Henry Bender, it was quite something. I have never experienced such a sight. I do not know what to think."

"Yes, I'm at a loss too. Hopefully, Father will know what it was."

"Yes, Father will know. Now, you must have something to eat and rest. Tomorrow we will go see him."

"Yes, you're right. I should rest up for tomorrow, as should you." I was learning to be as considerate in taking care of her as she had been in taking care of me.

In the morning, we found Father, as usual, sitting among his group. After describing what we saw, he looked at the others with a measure of surprise and said, "So… The Machine figured it out."

"Figured what out?"

"Henry, when The Machine was developed, they looked for a greater source of energy. An inexhaustible reservoir capable of regenerating itself so it would run forever. Mankind has always sought that capability. Despite making tremendous strides in developing limitless energy, they still fell short of finding the ultimate solution."

"However, until now, we assumed The Machine was operating on known energy sources. When our ability to do research was taken away, scientists were on the brink of a new discovery, said to be ahead of anything known before.

"What kind of power would not run out? Was it the sun, the wind, or was it atomic?"

"It was none of those. It was a new concept. It didn't yet even have a name. What you saw, I can only hope was the ultimate solution. From what I remember hearing about that project, it was to be an inanimate object, with no moving parts, made of a combination of elements that, when placed in saltwater, would draw in a limitless supply of energy from the ocean.

"The sun only provides power when it is out, the wind only when it blows, and atomic energy has its dangers. Also, this new energy wouldn't deplete its elements. Since none of us here had anything to do with that work, we know little else. Those who were engaged in it have long since departed."

"That's amazing. In my day, we would have given anything for that knowledge."

Father asked, "Sara, why did you and the children not tell us about those events taking place at the shore?" Hesitant to speak up, she said, "I am sorry, Father, but you know how the children are treated. All of them have been afraid of getting into trouble. And when I was a child, I was no different. However, we always assumed those events at the shore were known and not something to be reported."

"I did not know you felt that way," he said.

I said, "Yes, Father, there's a lot you don't know about Sara and the children."

"I see…"

I hoped he wasn't offended, for this was not the time for that sort of thing. Yet, I wondered why he didn't pick up what the children were thinking? Was I mistaken about them having a telepathic sense?

I asked, "Since we now found its source of power, will we be able to shut it down?"

"Henry, apparently, it only charges a small number of parts at one time, for we never noticed any appreciable number of parts missing for any length of time. Unfortunately, we do not know exactly what we're dealing with. We will have to examine the block and give it some thought."

"We can take you out in a boat."

"A boat? Henry Bender, what is a boat?" Sara asked.

"Henry, when I was young, I read about boats. But, since your times, as you can see, we have better forms of transportation. Boats are now mere artifacts."

"Okay, then we'll take you all out on a disk."

"Yes, after lunch, we will go and take a look," Father said, although, by his tone, I sensed a reluctance.

Later, on a disk large enough to accommodate the four of us, including Father's group of twelve, we flew to the ocean and hovered over the submerged block.

The children were still camped out on the cliffs, probably more so to have fun and do something different than anything else. I was astonished at how, with all its superior technology, The Machine could not sense all our additional activity. It seems the earlier reprogramming was effective. Even in my day, computers could spy on people. Then again, perhaps we are still the only ones capable of cognitive thinking, and it remains a fallacy to think a machine can do what we could do.

While on the disk, the group studied the block and then discussed it amongst themselves. I had not seen them so alive, but what they were saying was not part of my technical vocabulary. When they arrived at a consensus, the disk automatically flew to the cliffs and landed.

The children crowded around. It was clear how uncomfortable the adults were around the children. Perhaps that's the unfortunate result of not allowing natural bonding to be established.

I asked, "Father, what do you think?"

"In the original experiments, they were only able to create a tiny amount of energy. That knowledge was put into The Machine to expedite it, not long before it took over, and until now, only The Machine has known of the existence of the block."

Not really understanding how it was kept hidden for so long, I again asked the critical question, "Will we be able to shut it off?"

"We do not know. We need a sample to test."

"Can we safely get one?"

"You said it was lit up when it charged. We believe when it is dark, it has no charge and is safe to touch."

"You are saying, only at that time it can be touched?"

"We believe so but are not sure."

"So... Someone has to touch it to find out?"

"Yes, I'm afraid without test equipment, it is the only way."

"I guess that's my job," I hesitantly volunteered.

"No, not you!" Sara said with alarm. Roger, also alarmed, grabbed a black rock off the ground and smashed it against a larger rock, causing it to fragment into sharp edge pieces. He quickly picked the sharpest piece and took off on a disk flying out to the block before anyone could stop him.

Sara screeched, to no avail, "No, Roger!" I jumped on a disk and followed him. He plunged into the water with the rock in hand. Thankfully, within seconds, he emerged, holding up a tiny piece of the block. I hoisted him up onto my disk, and we flew back. He gave it to Father, who said, "You are a brave young man." Roger beamed with pride.

I marveled at Roger's know-how. Even though The Machine had taken away all of the tools, Roger figured out how to make a pre-historic cutting tool. Imagination was definitely still alive. I wondered how much more he would be capable of doing if he were free?

Father examined the piece and passed it around to his group. When it was back in his hands, he said, "We must take it back to where we can watch and study it."

Roger asked, "May I go with you?"

Father said, "Of course."

Sara and I weren't going to miss out either. We all mounted the large disk and headed to Father's unit.

I felt more than a tinge of hope that progress was finally being made.

CHAPTER 29 The Module

Back in Father's unit, he placed the fragment in front of everyone and just looked at it. He asked his group, "Who has any knowledge of this technology?" A couple raised their hands, and a technical discussion ensued. Again, I tried to follow along, but their technical language was entirely different from what I understood; it was like listening to Chinese.

They sat in silent meditation for a while. I was moved by seeing how their facial expressions changed for the better when dealing with a problem. I had almost given up on them, but now I saw there was still hope.

Father explained, "Those who worked on this had the theory, but not the way to carry it out. We surmise they could not find an ample supply of the substances needed to construct a block large enough to do the job. Their theory about the elements was apparently on the right track. Unfortunately, they only had enough time to produce a minute amount of what was needed. When they tested it in saltwater, it created only a spark from what any of us remember.

"They fed their discoveries into The Machine. However, before their involvement went any further, The Machine seized control and stopped their research. However, now we see The Machine continued that work on its own.

"After all these centuries, believing this technology was lost, it is a miracle to see it has come to fruition. Now, it will be our job to shut it down."

I asked, "If you do, would there be any power for us to use? I mean, would it be possible to disconnect just a part of it, for I'm sure we'll need a significant amount of energy to maintain the city?"

"Henry, this is why we need your input. We've been disabled for so long that it will take time for us to restore our full potential. Your mind is fresh. We need your logical thinking."

Wow. That was a significant boost to my ego, but I knew I only used simple logic and didn't deserve the praise.

Father turned to the group and asked, "Is there a way to disconnect part of it?"

I could almost feel their rusty minds beginning to work as I watched in awe. Before this moment, I hadn't fully appreciated how precious our minds were. Isn't it mystifying what life deals us? However, I was exhausted, mind, body, and spirit, yet I knew that even if I failed to help these people survive, I would've done my very best. I only wished Cecilia and Phil could've shared this experience with me; I missed them so.

The group began to discuss the possibilities, and as I watched, I realized I didn't really know these people. I don't even know most of their names, but destiny had brought us together. Our lives were now entwined; we had to work together for our survival depended on it.

It was a second chance at life given me—a true gift. Although I deeply miss my family and friends from my old life, I welcomed my new life. I looked at Sara with appreciation, knowing her care and concern replenished my existence. And to think this Machine would steal her soul! No, I must not let it happen. It must be shut down, or at least diverted from its sinister intent. When God created us, He didn't intend us to end up as a mindless pile of protoplasm.

Hmm… Where did that thought come from? I hadn't thought much about God since college. The group suddenly fell silent and looked at me. Sara grabbed my hand in anticipation.

Father said, "We believe there's a way. However, it must be tested."

Impatient, I said, "Well, let's do it."

Father said, "Yes, let's do it." It amused me to see his austere manner breaking down, for it was like seeing humanity being reborn.

He explained how the combination of the right elements, when dry, would sit dormant for eternity, but submerged in saltwater, it would soak up an unknown energy residing in the ocean that was believed to be unlimited and waste-free. They tried to explain how it worked, but it was still beyond me to understand their technical terms. Fortunately, I didn't need to know how it worked to deal with it, for they were here to help with the science.

I saw my primary job was to stimulate their minds. Their reliance on The Machine shut down the resiliency and purpose humanity once had. Incredibly, I was beginning to see how the erosion clearly first showed its ugly face in my day. I felt some guilt in knowing I had played an unwitting part in it. But this was not the time to be regretful.

Back then, people were enthusiastic about transferring their knowledge into computers. They believed it was a significant step forward. However, not much thought was given to what consequences might arise. I questioned why we were so willing to sell our souls in exchange for supposed convenience and comfort?

Some even believed that a person's very essence could be transferred into computers in addition to their knowledge. But I now see how computers, or machines as they now call them, are only capable of rote actions, for compassion and love come from a place only flesh and blood creatures can touch and connect with. Why would anyone want to give up their humanness in effect to become a machine?

Maybe, in a million years of development, this could be accomplished; but what purpose would it serve? These thoughts were coming at me all at once, almost as if someone was trying to tell me something. I had to sort it all out. Again this was not the moment.

I said, "Okay, Father. Tell me in the simplest terms—what must I do?"

"Henry, as you know, since The Machine cannot sense you, you are the only one who can get close enough without it sensing your intentions. Watch, I'll show you something." He placed the piece of the block in front of me and squeezed it, showing me it was as malleable as soft clay. But, when he let go, it returned to its original shape.

He explained, "It looks dormant, but it is not. It can draw in a substantial charge and release it in an instant. No other known material we know of is capable of this. As you can see, it can be squeezed, twisted, or even cut. We believe, if this piece were put back in its place, it would reconnect and mend into its original shape. It is impervious to damage.

"However, we believe for it to absorb and release that power, it would require some sort of on/off switch. When it is off, as it is now, it can be touched without danger. However, when in saltwater and the switch is flipped on, it draws in a vast amount of energy. And when it lights up, it is cable of releasing all that energy instantly. For anyone to touch it at that time, even you, it would be fatal.

"Our best calculations indicate the switch is not in the block. We believe it is in The Machine's module, which controls all of its functions. To gain access to the electronic switch, we must get through its defensive mechanism, which is also in the module. Unfortunately, we do not know where the module is located.

"You mean you don't know where its brain is?"

"Henry, I'm ashamed to say, we have not known where it has been for centuries. When it took control, it developed its own protection system, hiding the location of its brain—as you call it."

I asked, "Where could the module be, and what does it look like?"

"Henry, we are not sure, for its capabilities most likely have advanced well beyond our knowledge. However, we are convinced the block is only the storage unit and is controlled by the module. When we find it, the hope is we will be able to shut it down."

"Then we must find it."

"Henry, that is where your abilities come in. You come to this situation with a fresh perspective, and The Machine cannot detect you. You must help us find it."

Wow, what an extraordinary challenge! This was a far cry from the limited dangers my foolish stunts entailed. Now, I was faced with a real life-threatening situation. If not successful in conquering it, I fear the world as we know it would end. I had a vision of us all melting down into a liquid pool of humanity; what could be worse than that?

Yet, I couldn't complain, for it was the kind of challenge I longed for. A rush of fear and adrenaline shot through my body—I never quite understood how I could want something so bad yet feared it so.

The teachings I grew up with, which taught me about purpose, were beginning to make sense. At the same time, I must confess all this was overwhelming. Then again, I realized I couldn't let these people see my doubts. Thanks to my experience in out-bragging Phil and satisfying my old bosses, I felt I could convince them I knew what I was doing.

I asked, "Do you have any idea of what it looks like?" Father and the group discussed it, then said, "The last time it was seen, it could be held in one's hand, for most things were miniaturized long before our times. We suspect it's hidden in a protected area within the city."

Hearing that, it was hard to imagine something that size controlling an entire city with all its people. I asked, "Do you think the people will be able to help us look for it?"

"We do not know. Many have not been required to use their minds for hundreds of years."

"Do you think they have lost that ability forever?"

"To protect ourselves, we have kept a low profile for so long as if we were asleep. Consequently, we spent little time with the people and have no idea. However, the treated ones are no longer considered a threat to The Machine. Since they were neutralized, their chemistry remains unaffected no matter the circumstances."

I said, "To search the city, we're going to need all the help we can get."

Roger excitedly suggested, "The children could help too. Our minds are alert."

Sara added, "That would be wonderful."

"Great idea! Father, would it be permissible to send the children out into the city to help in the search?"

He looked to the others for a consensus and then said, "We have no experience with them. Do you think they can follow directions and remain calm? For if The Machine catches the notice of any of this, we are all doomed. Henry, what do you think?"

"I think they can handle it, and we're going to need everyone's help. It's going to take a lot of manpower to find this thing. Without the added help of the children's alert minds and the old people's cooperation, we might never find it. We have no choice, do we?"

"Then, everyone will help. That is what we will do. Henry, you are in charge," Father concluded.

With that edict, I took on the mantle of leadership, and boldly said to Sara and Roger, "Let's get busy. We must organize."

CHAPTER 30 Looking For A Way In

Sara, Roger, and I flew to the children's zone. As they gathered around, Roger impulsively announced, "We are going to destroy The Machine." Ominously, the children groaned.

I said, "Wait, let's not jump the gun." Although they didn't know what to destroy or what my comment meant, they fell silent. Sara and Roger helped me explain how in the morning, we were all going into the city. Splitting into small groups, we were to ask the old people if anyone had seen anything resembling the module. The only catch was not to mention the reason we were looking for it. And all had to be done with the least commotion possible. With the children's high energy, that would be a task in itself.

I knew it would not be easy for them, for they never were asked to do anything of consequence. In fact, it might be best if the children didn't understand what was going on. Still, there seemed to be no better choice to get this done. All we could hope was for them to be calm. As always, that night in my unit, Sara slept on the couch and I on my bed.

In the morning, we took only those children old enough to take part in the search. With any luck, the old people would remain placid as we asked them if they had seen anything unusual or hidden?

The simple act of asking questions seemed to stimulate the old people. Yet, they still didn't make eye contact and lacked the curiosity to ask what we were after. However, it was encouraging to see how they willingly joined in the search.

Many pointed to the spots they thought it might be hidden.

However, the pointing went in all directions. I saw it was going to take time, for every lead had to be checked until it was found.

Even in their condition, I could see an active communication system in play throughout the city, for the people seemed to understand we were looking for an unknown object before we asked.

Following up, the leads was tiring. By lunchtime, we found nothing concrete. Not sure if The Machine would feed the children within the city, Father ordered them to stand in line at the outdoor dispensing ports. I was relieved when it didn't distinguish them from the adults; each received their lunch. I again wondered if The Machine had any human intelligence. I was beginning to think not.

After the meal, I ordered the children not to put on their trainers as I had done before. They didn't seem to mind this time, for they were eager to get back to the search. Being their first time in the city, it was more like a game than a mission.

Surprisingly, no matter how much extra activity they created, it didn't disturb The Machine. Apparently, their positive attitudes added to the partial blocking. Still, in light of it all, it continued to baffle me, for I couldn't fathom how humanity had allowed this tragedy to occur.

In the afternoon, the children came across a man who had witnessed something of interest. It was the best lead so far. He claimed that he had seen a single lightning bolt strike the spire many times on top of Father's building in the dead of night. Each time it took only a second or two, perhaps just long enough to receive a massive energy charge.

Father said, "That is most interesting, yet it seems incredible it occurred right over our heads. However, it does make sense. I wonder why no one else noticed it."

I suggested, "Everyone here walks with their eyes cast down, never looking up. And perhaps, at that time of night, no one was still awake or alert enough to notice it."

"Ah, yes. That must be the reason."

"Henry, there's no access to go any higher than my unit."

"Father, have you ever checked out the floors above you?"

"We have always known the building rose well above us. And over the years, we attempted to search for it on our disks but were never able to approach the very top of my building. Come to think of it, that fact alone should've indicated it was a protected area.

"Wait… That would make it the perfect place to hide the module. How foolish we have been."

"Weren't you here to see the city being built?" I asked.

"No. The Machine had completed the city before anyone was allowed to enter. An army of drones kept the people away. And, since we moved in, we saw no need and have been afraid to explore too far in fear of revealing ourselves."

"I see."

After further discussion, it was concluded I was the only one who could get close enough to look. If it was up there, the group's calmness wasn't sufficient to allow them to come anywhere near enough to the top of the building.

The hope was it would allow me, an outsider, to take a look. Therefore, I nervously flew around its top. To my relief, it didn't repel my disk, as it had done with the others. Thankfully, The Machine still didn't consider me to be a threat. Therefore, I examined it close up with my architect's eye as if I didn't exist. There was a significant amount of unaccountable space above what they believed was the top floor. However, I didn't see any possible entry point short of breaking a hole in the wall.

Disappointed, I entered Father's space and examined the ceiling to find no visible access point there either. I said to Father, "Structurally, there's no reason or purpose for the unoccupied space above, except to hold up the spire and possibly the module."

"Henry, you've made your point, and I'm ashamed to admit that each time we were unable to get close, we pursued it no further due to our fear of discovery. Of course, if we knew of the spire being struck, it would have made a difference. If the control module is there, it has been concealed there since the city was built."

"I think it's time to find out."

"Yes, Henry, I agree. However, I must warn you again; The Machine's built-in protection system keeps unfriendly hands from getting too close, perhaps, even yours. If any of us rush in, it could cause a catastrophe."

"Are you able to disconnect it remotely?"

"When we were in control, we could. Again, regrettably, along with everything else, The Machine cut off our access to it."

"Father, what do you suggest?"

"Henry, first, we must make sure it is up there."

"Meaning someone has to look in there, right?"

Yes, and with your background and invisibility, you are the one to do it."I knew he was going to say that. The trouble was it made sense. However, I was unfamiliar with the material used in the building's construction. Sara saw my uncertainty and grasped my hand, saying, "Henry Bender, you are the only one who can do this."

Looking at the faces of the others, with their pleading expressions, how could I not try? However, if I could find a way in, I had to overlook my fear of death, which was no small matter. I was not in favor of losing my second life. However, despite that fact, I said, "I guess I am… Now let's make a plan." Although exhibiting a growing strength, Father and the group still showed indecisiveness. Seeing that, to accomplish anything, I had to display strong leadership. Even though I saw the doubt on their faces, it still gave me hope in seeing how dramatically their spirits had improved in such a short time.

We discussed the possible ways to look inside the upper structure without disrupting anything. They explained how the defense system most likely used sensing beams scouring the space to keep intruders out—the kind of thing I'd seen in action-adventure movies. At first, it seemed the only way to get in was to cut a big hole in the ceiling. However, when told of its defensive traps, it was decided it was too risky for that approach.

I rode around the tower again, looking even closer for any possible entry spots. I reexamined every inch of the inside ceiling and still found no breaches. Then I remembered this saying from my architect days, *if there's not a way in, there's no need for a way out.*

Consequently, the only option left was to cut a tiny hole just big enough to peek in as not to trigger its defenses. We all agreed it was the best and only approach.

After another extensive search, Sara looked me over and said, "Henry Bender, you need to rest."

"I'll be okay."

Father said, "Henry, you must not lose your strength. Without you, we will not succeed. It has been like this for hundreds of years. Taking a little more time will not do any harm." At that moment, without any doubt, I was highly stressed, and under these circumstances, I knew I had to relax.

Before leaving for the night, to keep the children involved, we sent them to the Wilderness knowing they were resourceful enough to find outdoor sleeping accommodations, for they enjoyed camping out. Sara and I went back to our unit.

As uptight as I felt, it was too early to sleep. Therefore, to occupy our time, I decided to see what more the book player had to say. Still curious, I asked about the period when the mass disappearance took place. A man's image began describing the one day when a quarter of the population vanished without a trace.

We both listened as he explained what the people of the time thought about that horrific event. Some believed the world was ending. Others thought it was the fulfillment of the Rapture. Hearing that, I realized religion was not yet dead

During the war's stress and his rule, "The One" turned people away from believing in the prophecy described in the biblical book of revelations.

That information gave me a new perspective on what happened. But, I was too weary to sort it out just then, and sleep overtook me.

CHAPTER 31 Organic Material

The next morning, Sara's sweet smile greeted me. I'd overslept which she allowed. I did appreciate it, but there was work to be done.

We started the day by heading to the Wilderness to check-in with the children. Sara was concerned about their well-being. In many ways, she was still childlike, and in other ways, she was the mother they needed. I hoped these people would find a way to reestablish the family structure. Perhaps the human spirit is more durable than it is given credit for.

The children were pleased to see us, eager to know what was next. Paradoxically, at this stage in their lives, they appeared to be a residue of my times. More so than a product of The Machine, as unlikely as that seemed.

As they gathered around, all I could tell them was to be patient and stay calm. As we were about to leave for Father's place, Roger asked, "Could we go with you?"

Sara immediately answered, "Yes, of course."

I smiled and said to all the children, "Come on, let's all go." In mass, we all flew off.

Once in the city, the children landed at Father's building base, while the three of us scooted up to the top floor. Father's group also seemed enthused to see us, which I considered another good sign; as they continue to look to me for direction. Having given it some thought, I asked, "Do you have any tools to cut a hole?"

One of them said, "The Machine took all our tools away."

I asked, "First, tell me exactly what material was used in

the construction of the building? It's like nothing I'd ever seen."

One answered, "It's an organic material The Machine grew."

That took me by surprise. Having figured it was a man-made product. I asked, "An organic material—you mean like a plant or a tree?"

"Yes. A concept developed long before The Machine existed. However, when it took over, it improved the process used to grow the city," Father said.

"You mean the city is growing? Even this building?"

"Not anymore. The Machine planted and grew the many structural elements in molds shaped in the forms needed. When grown to the size needed and still living, the pieces were placed in their prospective spots where the joints grew together, creating one solid piece. When it reached maturity, with all its joints secured and smooth out, its growth was stopped. Since then, the structure has remained the same size, stable and flexible for these hundreds of years. The Machine controlled the process. We know little else."

"Why, that's fantastic." I now understood why the out of plumb horizontal and vertical lines are so and had not collapsed. It's based on natural organic engineering, which is not within my expertise. I then realized that all those pillars holding up the city were, in fact, the trunks of trees. However, no one was able to explain why they were necessary. It seems only The Machine had that answer. I'll have to study it closer.

I asked, "Since there are no tools, what can I use to cut a hole in the ceiling?"

Father answered, "We'll have to find a sharp object. However, before you even try, you must consider The Machine's protection system. And if damaged by cutting a hole, instead of remaining dormant, it regenerates and repairs the intrusion, after which it becomes dormant again. Therefore it must be done quickly.

I asked again, "What can I use to cut a hole?"

"Henry, I must warn you again, many close friends have lost their lives as a result of trying to get close to The Machine."

"Father, all I can think of doing is to cut a hole just big enough to look in and see what the situation is. What do you think?"

"If the beam does not hit any of us directly, we believe The Machine will not be disturbed."

It was a task I wasn't looking forward to, but there seemed no alternative. Lacking any tools, it was not going to be easy. However, John said, "Did Roger not slit a rock into sharp pieces to cut the block?

"Yes, I have split many rocks," Roger said.

John said, "Roger, I'll go to the shore with you to get some of those rocks."

While they were away, Father and I carefully examined the ceiling. He chose what he thought to be the best spot to cut a hole. They soon returned with several split rocks. Selecting one, I chuckled at how we were using pre-historic sharp-edged rocks to combat the most advanced technology. Imagination was not yet dead.

I boarded a disk with the sharpest rock in hand and rose up to the chosen spot. With sweat dripping down my face, I had to mumble a prayer to nullify my extreme fear. If we guessed wrong, there would be shocking and possibly fatal consequences waiting above.

Incredibly, I was able to cut into the ceiling as if it were cheese. Chunking away, I cut a jagged round hole only inches across. As soon as I finished the incision, I quickly backed off. If The Machine were triggered, I didn't want to find out the hard way.

To my relief, nothing occurred. I saw the same relief in the others, especially Sara. Once assured, the sensors didn't spot the hole, I asked Father, "What's next?"

He bravely answered, "I'll have to look and see if it is in there."

"Are you sure?"

"Henry, we will be wasting our time if it is not there."

"Good point. Although, maybe I should look."

Henry, it is for me to do, for you do not know what to look for." On a disk, he rose up to the hole and looked in. By examining the visible light beams' direction and motion scanning the space, he calculated where the module might be.

With the aid of a small mirror mounted on a stick, handed to him by John, he manipulated it to spot the module. At the same time, he had to avoid the beams from reflecting off it.

It was impressive to see such an old guy exhibit such agility. I wondered where the mirror came from. Although guessing it was kept in the same secret place, they hid all the things they didn't want to be found.

He exclaimed, "Ah!" and came down, motioning for another man to look. After a third man looked, they nodded to one another. Father said, "It is there, as we suspected. From what we see of it, it looks to be the same shape and size as the module designed ages ago, although it most certainly has improvements. Since we haven't seen it for so long, we will need time to think about how to safely enter the space."

Not wanting to receive a shock again, I agreed. I then suggested, "I think the outside search should be called off."

Sara asked, "Father, do the children have to leave the city? They might be needed later."

I added, "The children need to be with adults."

"Then the children shall stay," Father ordered. "However, they must remain calm."

Roger volunteered, "I'll make sure they do" and happily flew off to do so.

Father suggested that while they contemplate how best to shut it off, everyone else should rest until they find a solution.

Sara took my hand, and we flew to ground level, leaving Father and the group to deal with the technical aspects, for it was too stressful to just watch while unable to help.

Roger had calmed the children as much as he could. We gathered them into another flotilla and led them to the Wilderness, for it seemed the best place for them to expend their energy without causing any problems while still being around old people.

As the children romped about, Sara and I went for a walk. I said, "Sara, when I was young, my parents taught me all things happen for a reason. However, everything in this world makes little sense. In my youth, I developed a false sense of confidence, which was necessary to succeed in my world. However, even now, I feel insecure, for I could've never imagined, not even in my wildest dreams, being in a situation like this."

I assumed she had no idea how unsure I was, or did she? At times I felt she was reading my mind and understood more about me than I gave her credit for. In my former life, I tried not to reveal my insecurities, especially to Cecilia. I felt if I showed my inner self, I would've lost her for sure. Something I was never able to admit.

With Sara, it is the opposite. She made me feel comfortable with who I was. I don't fear she would abandon me because of my weaknesses. I don't understand why I feel that way about her, for it seemed risky. But it allows me to let my defenses down. Despite everything, she always comforted me and gave me a boost.

Yet, at the same time, I still had a tiny glimmer of hope all this was only a dream, although I knew it was all too real. In a way, I wished I could wake up and be with Cecilia and Phil, for I missed them so... But on the other hand, Sara made me feel like the man I was comfortable with being, and if I lost her, I know I would miss her more than anything else.

Regardless of those conflicting feelings, I had to face the reality of the moment. Tiring, we sat on one of the benches. I asked, "Tell me something more about yourself?"

"Henry Bender, there's nothing more to tell."

"There must be. Did you grow up like the other children?"

"Yes, all children grow up the same way."

"You have no family structure? I mean, no mother or father?"

"As I said, all older women are our Mothers, and Father is our father. I do not know anything else."

As I listened, I began to see how my day's social conditions could've been the germ that contributed to this heartbreaking situation. The mantra was to do your own thing. People were expending their energy protesting this or that at all times. When I was there, I hadn't given social thinking enough thought. Although I was aware of what the opposing factions were saying through the media, I didn't connect with it. I was doing well and didn't want to get involved in anything controversial.

I felt compelled to share my inner thoughts with her because she was my only connection to the thread of life still remaining for me. I had a compulsion to share the wrongs of my day as if I had the power to make things right. I never worried about freedom in my former life, for I thought it was just there and would always be there. I had felt little or no responsibility to talk about it. But now, it seems that responsibility has become mine alone.

I took her hand and said, "I would like you to understand something." Looking at me in wonder, maybe not knowing what to think, yet she seemed pleased.

"Henry Bender, what is it you want me to understand."

I saw in her eyes the innocence that perhaps Eve had in the Garden of Eden. At that moment, I had the unfathomable feeling we were the only two people left on earth. It was almost a spiritual experience. I said to her, "People were not meant to be mindless and not in charge of their destiny."

"Henry Bender, what are you telling me?"

I wasn't sure how to explain what I was feeling. I was experiencing flashbacks from my past that taught me to think the way I do, instead of how these people thought. I now understood what happens when people surrender their natural birthright as human beings, whether it's to a dictator or a machine as they had done.

In my day, we were racing forward so fast we felt it was necessary to turn more and more tasks over to computers. But we didn't think it through; we relied on many unproven concepts. As I began to think more deeply about these issues, I recalled some of the teachings I was taught as a child, including the Bible books, and saw no sign of that knowledge left in this world. What happened to humanity's faith?

I asked her, "Have you ever heard of the Bible?"

"The Bible? Why, no. What is it?"

I knew these people had given up those beliefs ages ago. In my opinion, they discarded some of the very elements that gave people purpose, and as a result, it caused humanity to end up in this predicament. Consequently, I began to teach her about family life by first telling her the story of Adam and Eve. I related it at the most basic level, for I was never a great student of it.

She didn't know what to make of their man/woman relationship. I didn't push it, for I hoped in time, she would come to understand. Actually, I feared these people's biology might have forever changed to their detriment.

As she listened, her eyes lit up; it was encouraging. Her interest kept my hope alive. I continued to feel the human spirit was not yet dead. I saw in her and Roger that humanity was worth saving, even if there were only a few of them left. Wasn't it written, *"If only ten good people were left, the city would not be destroyed?"* I must look that up.

As Father and the group made their calculations, which I saw they were in no rush to do, I began telling stories to Sara and the children of their long-forgotten heritage.

Since I hadn't paid enough attention to the concepts I was taught in my youth, I realized I needed to restudy it. Therefore, I watched and listened to the holograms who told of the origins of the human race, in which I couldn't leave out the books of the Bible.

Even though the society of my day eventually collapsed, I believed those old stories still have significance. Therefore, I watched the books from those times, hoping I could use their ideas and messages to build a new society.

I speculated that the quickest way to give hope and purpose back to these people was through the children. Only this time around, they must not allow it to be corrupted. As they watched and listened to the holograms telling the stories, I saw miraculous changes taking place in their perspectives. I never appreciated the value of those stories before. Those ones that taught morality and ethical behavior, which drove me to continue. Was being a teacher my true calling?

CHAPTER 32 Revelation

A couple of days passed without a word from Father or his group. Growing impatient, Sara, Roger, and I went to see how things were coming along.

Father greeted us and filled us in. Explaining how, after much discussion, they had come to the conclusion that the security system was both deadly and impenetrable. Looking for answers, they had been catching up on their knowledge, for it had been so long since they were required to think of such things. Despite their hard work, I could tell they were hesitant and needed more evidence before taking action.

Therefore, I suggested the next time the block recharged, they come and see. However, I again saw a reluctance with my proposition. I was taken back a bit. If not willing to take action, how could they ever expect to break free of The Machine's control? It appears after hundreds of years in hiding, they had developed such an ingrained fear of being more visible to The Machine. This was unacceptable. Having lived in freedom, I saw it was going to be up to me to show them how to exercise it. I saw the need to give it my best sales pitch.

Although having lived in a free world, I also restricted myself, especially in my career. Therefore, in a way, this was new ground for me too. Yet, I urged them to act. Telling them this might be their only shot at breaking free.

Thankfully, Father conceded. "Henry, you are correct. The next time the charging occurs, we will go with you." With that settled, we left them to continue their work.

In the following days, I held study sessions with the

children. We examined their history and sound reasoning. Feeling a bit rusty myself, I did my best to disseminate information as I remembered it. Unexpectedly, for the first time, I was beginning to equate the New Testament and sound thinking as being the same. In a way, this was a new concept for me.

We found holding gatherings in the Wilderness was the best place for learning, as much as it was for the old as it was for the young.

I found flaws in my own thinking. I was beginning to see how our collective thinking had become lopsided. In denying our spiritual side, we gave that infinite power away. These people knew little of that power. In fact, all they knew was their tiny island—nothing more.

The disks couldn't, or perhaps wouldn't, travel much beyond the shoreline. Then again, it could've had something to do with The Machine's control. Maybe The Machine knew there was something more out there and didn't want anyone to learn about it. Or was it as simple as having a fear of traveling to explore beyond that point?

However, I felt confident there had to be other populated places and wondered if the cultures were similar. I looked forward to investigating those possibilities. But for now, I had to keep my focus on the immense threat at hand.

As I reflected, I was beginning to understand how, in my day, society was already collapsing. Now, the question was, what will it take to construct a new one. Without a stable social structure, these people would quickly again fall prey to those who would dominate.

While watching and listening to the old inspiring stories, whether they were based on truth or fiction, I saw it was as good or better than any other structure to date. It was what had worked from the beginning of humanity that taught people how best to act. It was almost magical how fast the children grew in their understanding and acceptance; even the old people seemed to pay better attention as they listened. I could see how imagination and spirituality were embedded in our genes.

When I saw how this knowledge enlivened these people, I realized that all people, in one way or another, follow what others said before them in storytelling. In my day, many vigorously believed their thoughts were entirely original. I must admit I also fell into that trap.

They didn't understand by studying their history was in their best interests. Instead, they invented and relied on untested concepts. I can now see how they lost their way by believing their generation was the smartest ever. For them, not to look at the accumulated body of knowledge only misguided them, and I was one of them. I could only think if one had gone back thousands of years, they would've found more common sense than many had in my day.

Sara asked, "Henry Bender, what is bothering you?" She knew my state of mind, for I couldn't hide a thing from her.

"I once had a decent life and enjoyed using the technology of my day. Seeing where it has led us devastates me knowing that humanity might end because of it. Can you understand what I'm trying to say?"

"Henry Bender, I never thought of such things before. However, I am beginning to see things as you do."

I was moved by seeing her growth. Yet, I also saw her weaknesses due to her being subservient to The Machine. Suddenly, as if from left field, a thought struck me, and I said, "That's what it has to be!"

Startled, Sara asked, "What does it have to be?"

"What happened to those people who disappeared in that one day at the beginning of the Great War has to be true."

"What happened to them?"

"I can't prove it, but it's beginning to fit together. I was never much into theology. But wait... let me play this for you." I played the book of Revelation. Knowing how difficult it was to understand, I explained, "You see, The Great War was going to be so bloody that God took his people up in the rapture, saving them from the pain and suffering that was to happen, as He promised he would at the end of time."

As I said, I could hardly believe what I was experiencing. I saw why Revelation had to take place. It was God's way of saving His chosen ones from the awful times mankind was about to inflict on itself.

"Sara, I know this might sound crazy, but what else could've happened to those people who disappeared?"

She asked, "What about those left behind?"

I then realized the real losers were those who survived the war and remained behind. They never understood what took place. Regrettably, I said, "I'm afraid those left behind likely thought of themselves as being good, but unfortunately didn't make the grade. Sadly, their descendants are now suffering from their mistakes." Startled, I was struck by the question, why is this world still here? I had believed it was to be over at the end times.

Distressed to hear this, she asked, "What does it all mean, and what is going to happen to us?"

I saw I was upsetting her and said, "Don't worry; when The Machine is shut off, things will get better." She smiled, and I understood I had to take a different tact, for I didn't like seeing her upset. Although, I strongly felt that she, along with all the others, had to understand what happened to them.

I didn't understand it all either. I had to explain my thinking and said, although, much of it was speculation on my part. "You see, after the war and the dark times, those who survived began to rebuild, only they hadn't learned the lessons, for they didn't grasp that they were still on the wrong path. What they had lost was the guidance and wisdom that taught people right from wrong.

"Without understanding their purpose, most people became unwittingly convinced it was best to sacrifice their souls for the sake of what they believed was progress."

I had to consider all this was too much for her to handle? In fact, I had to accept, under those circumstances, I was now also a loser, which troubled me to my core. I continued to wonder why the world and these people still existed? Despite what was prophesied.

However, she then asked, "You mean there are others than The Machine who punish?" I was surprised at that insight. I believed she was beginning to understand being controlled by The Machine was not good. Yet I realized, regardless of these people still being here, they desperately needed to expand their understanding. I could only think there has to be a good reason for them to have remained.

Again, I asked her, "If they understood what The Machine was doing, why didn't they stop it?"

"As Father said, The Machine had control, and, for it to maintain its reign, it treated anyone who defied it."

"Yet, you and those around Father were not?"

"Yes. As you know, we learned how to remain calm."

As many times as I heard that excuse, it was still incomprehensible, for that explanation of why these things took place was too simplistic. Even in my day, there were warning signs against computerization. Yet, people still willingly turned their lives over to computers without counterbalancing it with their human or, more clearly, their spiritual side, which is the main component now missing that once gave humanity substance.

"I wish I could learn what your times were like," She lamented.

"I'll teach you all about it."

"Yes, Henry Bender, especially about intercourse."

Now… That stopped my train of thought dead in its tracks. Despite not being quite as beautiful as Cecilia, she was still very appealing. She had such a sweet and gentle soul; how could I not be attracted to her? In fact, being close to her gave me a deep feeling of peace. Something I hadn't ever felt before, even with Cecilia.

I said, "I'll get to that." I knew family life was something she had to learn about; I just wasn't yet sure how to discuss it with her.

However, she moved close, touching me, looking into my eyes, and saying, "Show me?"

Wow! Even in my weakened state, and not knowing if I could even function in that capacity, I couldn't help but move closer to her. However, I quickly concluded—what the heck; we might not live another day in this crazy world.

Impassioned, and not considering anything but gently kissed her warm lips, which led us to join in intercourse. To my great pleasure, that act seemed to also cause pleasure in her, at least I'd hoped it was. It was like nothing I'd ever experienced before.

To my delight, I was still able to function, although not as robustly as I once had. I thought it was great sex with Cecilia, but this was in another dimension. It seemed all the pent-up abstinence of humanity released in her all at once; she embraced me with wild abandonment. Although I'm probably overstating her responses. I wanted it to go on forever. However, in time, after several rounds, from sheer exhaustion, we fell asleep in each other's arms.

With her still in my arms. when I awoke in the morning, I wondered what she thought of our night together

She awoke and asked, "Henry Bender, was that intercourse?"

"Yes, it was."

"I never felt that way before, and I want to do it again." I chuckled and embraced her, and we did it again.

After a much-needed period of recuperation, for she took everything out of me, she cheerfully asked, "Henry Bender, what is there to be done today?"

"Sara, I think we need to visit Father."

"Yes, let's go."

CHAPTER 33 Sara's Exuberance

Arriving in Father's unit, Sara immediately said, "Father, I found out what intercourse is. Can we show you?"

Staggered… I had to think fast. I grabbed her hand, saying, "Excuse us…" I took her onto a disk and flew to the wooded area in the Wilderness.

She asked, "Henry Bender, what is troubling you?"

I understood how, in her innocence, she had no idea what she had done. Nevertheless, I had to let her know that one's sex life was a private matter. Before I spoke, I took a few deep breaths to calm down, for it was one of the most embarrassing moments in my life.

I began to explain it in the kindest way I could, "Intercourse is the most special thing a man and woman do together and is not to be shared with anyone else. Whatever we do when we come together in love is just between us." Maybe, I was being prudish, but that's the way I viewed it.

She listened carefully, then said, "Henry Bender, I am sorry. I just wanted to tell Father how good I felt. I will not do it again." She then asked, "Henry Bender… What is love?"

"Sara, that would take some time to explain. However, if we stayed away too long, Father would wonder what happened to us. Right now, we must get back. I'll explain love when we're alone and have the time."

"Yes, Henry Bender, but first, could we have a little intercourse?"

"Oh… My-o-my. She is going to wear me out, but how could I refuse her warmth? After the quickest quickie ever.

Shamelessly, for she was faster than I was, we headed back to see Father.

Upon our return, he asked, "Henry is everything all right?"

She quickly said, "Everything is beautiful." Father smiled.

I quickly changed the subject, "Father, how are things developing?"

Henry, we believe The Machine's weakest moment is just before it receives a new charge. If we intercede and block it, it will be our best chance for success. Do you agree?"

Not really understanding how it all worked, I said, "It sounds good to me."

"Good. Then let's have something to eat."

That sounded good too. After the side excursion with Sara, I was extra hungry.

When we finished eating, I broached the subject I was itching to discuss, for it had been gnawing at me. I was careful, for I had no idea where these people stood as far as their spiritual beliefs were concerned, and I've come to believe that's where the missing element was. At the same time, I couldn't rationalize why it had become such a concern to me.

Despite it, I said, "I've been wondering more and more about what caused all those people to disappear on the same day at the beginning of The Great War. After giving it a lot of thought, I've arrived at a conclusion."

Sara added, "Yes, Henry has been deep in thought about this." I loved that in her, for I never knew anyone who had so much faith in me.

Father said, "Henry, tell us what you found," as everyone looked at me and waited.

"First, may I ask if you have a belief system?" In my day, it was a controversial and divisive subject, which I avoided discussing. But now felt I had to tackle it.

They looked at one other in silence, which I interpreted as they weren't sure what I meant, or perhaps there was something they didn't want to tell me. However, I took the chance and bluntly asked, "Have you ever heard of the Bible?"

Father then said, "We know in the times before The One came, people followed many different beliefs. As I recall from my studies, the Bible depicted one of them. It told of a man who came in peace and love to save the world."

"What does your history say about him?"

John asked, "Was he not killed to pay for the sins of the world?"

"Yes, he was. But... First, tell me more about the person you called The One?" Having an awful premonition of who he was, as I recalled from those teachings in my youth.

"Henry, from what I remember, at first, he was a man who also came as a person of peace and love. However, once he gained total control, he outlawed all other beliefs, especially the Bible. He not only attacked those who did not follow his edicts but persecuted all those who did not bow to him. His extreme actions led to the Great War. After his death, because of the devastation he caused, people were confused and not willing to return to any of the old beliefs."

"Did The One have a name?"

"He did, but since he caused so much harm, his name was obliterated and was never to be spoken again. Consequently, his name is no longer known."

"I see... And the Bible was not spoken of either?"

John said, "Yes. People felt that since the God of the Bible could not protect them from the war, they could no longer trust it."

I saw how this could get tricky, for I wasn't knowledgeable enough, and I didn't want to confuse or pressure them. Apparently, these people had some knowledge of the Bible but no longer used it as a reference point in their lives. Aside from that, it troubled me these people had no actionable way to set them free. They lost sight of that path despite it being right there for the taking. Their only concern was reduced to the basic instincts of survival. As human beings, they deserved better than that. Again, theoretically, flesh and blood people shouldn't be here any longer. Were they only figments of my imagination? That's a scary thought.

None the less, I couldn't help myself and asked, "What if the Bible predicted the war and your fate thousands of years ago?" They seemed skeptical yet intrigued. I suggested they listen along with me to Revelation's book since I thought it would explain it better than I could. I was taking a big gamble, for I wasn't sure how they would react. However, they agreed to do so.

While the narrator spoke, I observed them as they intensely watched and listened. When over, after a momentary silence, Father said, "We never knew of this. Was it describing The Great War? And did it say, when those people disappeared, our people were the ones left behind?"

That was insightful, and I could only say, "It would seem so?" Seeing their disheartened expressions, I quickly said, "But, it doesn't mean all is lost." Perhaps I was too presumptuous, for understanding the message Revelation implied was challenging, to say the least.

"Henry, what do you mean, all is not lost?"

I realize, not being well prepared it can get out of hand. So I decided to cut it short and said, "Before we discuss anything else, we must first defeat The Machine and set you free."

Sara jumped in and said, "Then, that is what must be done."

Father said, "Sara, I see that is so." As all those in the room looked at each other and nodded in agreement, to my relief. Again, I couldn't help but feel there was something they weren't telling me.

A lengthy discussion followed about the options open to us concerning The Machine. After which, Sara said, "Henry Bender needs to rest." I was still not in favor of her highlighting my weaknesses. However, the truth was, after the discussion and the physical exuberance with her, I was drained. Sara always knew when I reached that point.

I was beginning to let go of my need to uphold any macho status. Those symbols were losing their meaning to me. Perhaps I was finally growing up.

Sara and I headed to our unit.

CHAPTER 34 Finding Direction

Back in our unit, it struck me; perhaps the answers I sought were long ago embedded in the Bible, for nothing else in this world made better sense. Compelled to look for those answers, I asked the player about the meaning of life. A hologram of a different man rose up. I was getting used to seeing those individuals but wondered who they once were, for there were no descriptions given.

As Sara and I watched and listened, I saw a thread developing I felt was leading to an answer. When it was over, I said, "Let's look at another one."

She said, "No, Henry Bender, you need to rest."

"I can't sleep."

"Henry Bender, may I help you?"

"Okay. Do it." She tapped the pad, the beam touched my head, and I was asleep.

The next morning, I thought about how Roger let us know when the first parts showed up at the beach. Sara just knew when they arrived. Yet, for some unexplained reason, I hesitated in asking about it.

At breakfast, I finally asked her to explain that apparent ability.

She said, "I thought you knew. You see, from the people we are connected with and trust, we can receive what they want us to know."

"And you do this without speaking? You mean, telepathically?"

"I do not know what that word means or how to explain

what takes place. It is just the way it has been."

I said, "I see," realizing I wasn't going to get a clear answer. Again I could only wonder; with that added extra sense, why has so much gone wrong? I'll have to ask Father about that.

She asked, "What is there to do today?"

I suggested we go and see the children, for there was a lot more I wanted them to know.

She said, "I will tell them we will meet them in the Wilderness."

"You mean by a telepathic message?"

"If that is what you call it, then yes."

I couldn't help but be astonished by that ability. Nonetheless, I took the book player, and we headed out.

Once there, I played other books for the children. Upon watching and listening, they asked many questions, which I answered the best I could. The children had the most difficulty with the concept of other things being more important than The Machine. In essence, these people accepted The Machine as their god, although they didn't understand that imagery. People had lost sight of the God I understood.

The question was, could I help restore some semblance of what humanity once was? I was convinced what was needed was a spiritual awakening to find purpose again. They needed something to connect with, not in fear, but in love, to propel them to a fuller life.

Not everyone from my day would've agreed with how I was handling this. But I concluded what was needed was a solid foundation to live by. Understanding from my limited life, I reasoned the Bible was as good a start as any. Not to overlook, The Machine was still our immediate concern. I wished I could expedite shutting it down, but I had to wait for Father's tactical direction.

If I didn't have Sara's warmth to relax in, I might have

walked away from this overwhelming burden. Yet, on the other hand, I believed, if there is a God, it might be possible to get back in His grace. Without having indisputable evidence of His existence in this lost world, it still seemed logical to fall back to His teachings. Otherwise, why, after Armageddon took place, did He allow humanity to continue? It was something not written about. Maybe, it was not beneficial to be known?

I was far from having confidence in any of my conclusions. But I felt compelled and motivated to follow this path, for it looked like humanity was, without some sort of powerful intercession, on the road to extinction.

Sara asked, "Henry Bender, what is troubling you?"

I could only answer with a question. "Do you understand what I'm saying when I talk about my God?"

"Yes, Henry Bender. Your god is like The Machine."

Despite my frustration, I was pleased to see she was learning, for that statement was a step forward, but there was much work ahead. I said, "Only there's a significant difference; my God represents love, and The Machine has none."

"Henry Bender, there's that word love again, which you have not explained."

"You're right... I'd forgotten." At that point, I wasn't sure I could explain it well enough, but I felt it was necessary to at least try, and said, "You see, love applies to many things in different ways. It's about how we feel about and treat each other..."

She interrupted, "How do we feel about each other?"

"What do you mean?"

"I mean, with love."

"Well, love is about caring for each other, wanting to be close, and missing the other when apart."

"Do you care about me? Do you miss me when apart? Do you love me?"

Wow. I guess I walked right into that one. Whether she knew it or not, she was calling for a commitment. However, it took me only a second to reflect. I wasn't surprised how easy for me to say, "I do."

"Show me."

Oh my, here we go again. Although I was pleased to see her catching on.

CHAPTER 35 The Great Shutdown

Sara urgently said, "Roger wants us to come to the shore."

"That telepathy thing again, right?"

"Yes, it is."

"Do you hear him speaking?"

"No, I just know. I cannot explain it."

Father also got the message, and along with his group, arrived shortly after we did. All the children were at the cliff's edge, captivated by what was taking place on the beach. There were a small number of disks with a Machine part clearly piggybacked on each one. Only this time, instead of all the disks connected to one another, only the piggybacked parts were joined to one another, which created the one circuit waiting to be charged.

I asked Father, "What do you think it's doing?"

"It appears to be newly made parts brought here to receive their first charge."

They were weird-looking pieces of equipment. No one part was the same, having a variety of different shapes and sizes. I asked if he knew what they would be used for?

Father consulted with the group and then said, "Henry, we do not know; some of the designs were never seen before. It might be to deal with us as the drones did in the past. If that is so, it is not a good sign."

"Do you mean it knows what we're up to?"

"Again, we do not know, for its communications do not speak of its intentions. It only states the present facts. However, we do believe our time is running out, and we must act soon."

His concern was alarming; I had to think fast. "Father, didn't you say we should be with the module at the right moment to shut it down?"

As if it hadn't occurred to him until I mentioned it, he said, "Yes, it is wise to be with the module." He ordered, "The children will stay here to give us notice while we go to be with the module."

I looked at Sara and asked, "They'll give notice by that telepathy thing, right?" Still finding it hard to believe. She smiled and nodded a yes. We headed to his penthouse with Father's group—as I now preferred to call his place.

When there, Father cautiously peered into the hole I'd cut. It had grown a little smaller, and I could only wonder, since the city had stopped growing, how was it still capable of repairing itself?

He instructed, "When the time comes, we will have to act fast. We believe that it briefly turns off its sensors to receive a new charge. We must seize that fleeting moment. It will be our only opportunity to get close enough to safely touch it and shut it down. We will need to submerge it in water before it turns back on. Henry, how can we best accomplish this?"

I saw this was a do-or-die situation, and I had to get it right. Fortunately, there was time to prepare. I ordered, "First, we will cut a groove in the shape of a big round hole, big enough for Father and John to fly in. However, we'll cut it only deep enough as not to break away and fall down on its own for the time being. When the right moment arrives, we will quickly break it open to allow them to fly in."

Unfortunately, I could only guess what depth the cut should be for it not to break prematurely. Although risky, I couldn't see how else to do it. Roger and I rose to the ceiling, and with the sharp rocks, we quickly began to slice away a groove about two-thirds of the ceiling's thickness. I was thrilled how easy it was to cut into it. I found it incredible how that soft material was able to support the weight of the ceiling. But it did.

When finished, I was able to breathe again, relieved the piece didn't separate. I said, "Okay, everybody. When the time comes, we will open that hole. Father and John will fly in and grab the module and hand it off to Roger and me, who will fly to the Wilderness and dunk it in the lake to short-circuit it. Does everyone understand and agree?" They all nodded, even though their understanding and agreement were not needed.

I said to Sara, "You should leave the building."

She said, "Where you will be, I also will be."

Again seeing her resolve, I said, "Ok, but please stay on the opposite side of the room." She acknowledged she would.

There was nothing left to do but to wait, and being so stressed, it was not going to be easy. The elders took turns watching through the hole, looking for any changes. Meanwhile, we ate, napped, and talked to one another about having faith, for this was a time it was most needed.

When darkness fell, as usual, the building's interiors were well-lit. It was amazing how there were no lamps or other visible sources where the light was coming from, yet, a radiant glow filled those spaces. This city never ceased to astound me.

As the night crept on, we remained ready. Roger and I were given a few of those lights on a cord to hang around our necks. I grew impatient, almost reaching the point of feeling I couldn't take it any longer. Finally, a message was received from the cliffs that it was beginning—the block was rising. We mounted our disks; I couldn't help but cross my fingers and mumble a little prayer.

The wait was unbearable, although it was only minutes before Father ordered the go. We moved quickly, breaking away the prepared section. Father and John sailed through it. They frantically examined the module, which surprisingly was no larger than a pack of cigarettes with nothing connected to it.

They handed it to Roger and me, and we flew it to the lake at a breathtaking speed.

Within seconds we were hovering at the edge of the water, lighting the area with our lamps. Unseen by us, the block had lit up and began to rise. Roger received instructions to dump the module in the water before it was able to receive the charge. We then flew to what we thought was a safe distance and waited with extreme anxiety. We weren't sure if it would work, and if it didn't, we had no clue what would happen.

However, almost immediately, Roger knew the block went dark and sank back down into the ocean. Hopefully, The Machine was now defenseless. Was it that simple? However, that was the easy part. Now, Father's team had to figure out how to restart it, only this time under their control.

Roger exclaimed, "We must quickly bring the module to Father." Oh, how I envied his telepathic ability! I fetched it from the clear water, and we sped back.

Returning, we found Father's group in the thoroughfare outside the building and gave him the module in the light of their individual lamps. They opened it and began studying its circuitry. As they worked, we were left with nothing to do. Sara and I desperately needed to relax and had to get away from the tension. We flew to the Wilderness. Yet, once there, all we could think about was what was going to happen next.

Sara asked, "Henry Bender, do you think they will be successful?"

"I certainly hope so. But if not, I believe things will work out one way or the other, for people are resourceful." I hoped that optimism was justified.

"Henry Bender, I have never known life without The Machine being in control. What is it going to be like?"

"Sara, if one does the right things, it can be great."

"What are the right things?"

"Don't worry. I'll teach you." I gave myself another tall order, for humanity has always struggled with that question. Indeed, in my life, I hadn't always made the best choices.

However, I was given a second chance, and I was determined to make it count.

"Henry Bender, I know you will." At that moment, I loved her so and only hoped we would survive long enough to have a meaningful future together. Exhausted, we soon fell asleep in each other's arms.

CHAPTER 36 A New Beginning

The next morning, fortunately, the food dispensing ports still had stored power to supply breakfast. Although we knew, if they couldn't successfully restart it, we would soon go without. We boarded a disk and headed to the penthouse.

We found Father and his group still at ground level, huddled around the disassembled module. They'd spent the night puzzling over how to make the corrections, which would allow the reprogramming to activate.

A lot was riding on their success, for if they failed, all the assets within the distribution system would be unreachable, as there was not enough room for people to squeeze through the labyrinth. The disks would also run out of their stored power, leaving us unable to fly over the mountains

Father said, "Henry, we think we figured out what to do. We believe we've located the sections The Machine added to the original circuitry, which allowed it to become independent. Although we have no testing equipment, it is evident those additions were not designed by our people. By removing those alien circuits, The Machine should now be as it was when it was first put into service so long ago."

"Won't it try to take over again?" I asked.

"Not if we keep control of the programming. The critical mistake was in willingly handing over that control. In a few minutes, we will be ready to turn it on to see if it accepts our corrections."

It was remarkable how they could accomplish this without tools; they simply picked it apart with their bare hands, and by using Roger's sharp rocks, they severed the trouble spots.

It was now like waiting for a miracle. If successful, it would wipe out a thousand years of destructive history. Humanity would have a fresh start. As we waited, Sara tightly clenched my hand.

The children were on the cliff, watching the block for signs of movement. Finally, with it patched up and dried off, Father closed the module's lid, turning it on. We all moved back to what we thought was a safe distance, not really knowing.

Now being daylight, we feared its timing was out of sync. Therefore we hoped upon hope that something would happen well before nightfall.

Time passed, and, just as our hopes were beginning to wane, Father exclaimed, "The block is rising!"

Suddenly, above the city, lightning bolts flashed in all directions with a mighty raw. Then, everything ceased—but not for long. We all watched as one gigantic bolt of energy struck the spire atop Father's building and dramatically bounced off down to the module with us at a safe distance.

Father raised his hands to quiet everyone. In the silence, as they closed in around it, it began to beep. Father listened until it stopped and then turned to me, declaring, "It is done. The city is energized. We are free." Although still zombie-like, the people began to stir as a thunderous cheer broke out from the masses.

Father, transitioning us out of the excitement and back into reality, said, "The real task begins now; most of us have not done anything like this for centuries. Henry, since you are the one who understands the work it will take, you must lead the way. Tell us what is next?"

I was overwhelmed as Sara squeezed my hand with a twinkle in her eyes, saying, "Yes, you can do it.

Not wanting to disappoint her, I took a gulp of air, cleared my throat, and said, "As Father said, now the work begins. I come from a time of hope and freedom, a time when people valued truth, honor, strength, responsibility, goodness, and above all, love. Sadly, we never fully achieved all those values, but we had the freedom to try.

"Now that you're free, you must also try. In the past, by relying on The Machine, you gave away your birthrights. You've missed out on the right to make your own choices, work, love, respect, and take care of one another. You must now understand that living without a purpose is not living at all. With this new beginning, you must choose to work towards embodying those values. Let's not abandon them again; let's work to restore your dignity."

Upon saying that, I couldn't imagine where my words came from, yet they flowed out of my mouth. This experience was new to me, having always avoided public speaking. But magical changes were taking place. And it felt great to express such profound thoughts.

Yet, as good as I felt, it was daunting; it seemed the weight of the world was on my shoulders. In their state, I knew these people couldn't fully comprehend most of what I said, for I wasn't sure I fully understood it myself. Yet, another cheer burst out.

I was encouraged, for I saw a new spirit emerging. Experiencing all this exhausted me. Of course, Sara knew this, and turned to Father and said, "Henry Bender must rest now."

Father said, "Yes, you must rest so that you are prepared for what tomorrow will bring."

Sara always knew when to bow out, and we did.

CHAPTER 37 The
Reawakening

With the sweet smell of freedom in the air, Sara and I decided to detour and spend the night in the Wilderness. I much preferred camping out to being pent-up in my lackluster unit.

We landed in a secluded area by the lake. Later, relaxing under a magnificent starry sky, we couldn't help but make love again, after which we fell asleep in each other's arms.

The next morning, in our newfound world, we skinny-dipped in the lake. Sara had never done anything like that before; in fact, she'd never even undressed in front of others. Just like all the people of her time, she wore her coveralls twenty-four-hours a day. When we made love was her first time being naked in front of another person.

Trying our best to be discrete, we entered the water under cover of the woods. The crystal-clear lake gave us both such an incredible feeling of release. These people had no idea what they were missing. Advancement is not always what it's cracked up to be. The simple things in life, such as eating, sleeping, working, achieving something good, enjoying others and the surroundings, and sharing love, make life worthwhile.

After spending the morning there, immersed in the simplicity of our joy, I felt pangs of hunger. We headed out to have breakfast with the children.

It was interesting to see that they decided to remain in their area. I'd hoped their new freedom would lead them to be more adventurous and curious about city life. I envisioned them mixing with the adults, creating new bonds. I then realized those relationships were going to take time to develop.

During breakfast, Roger asked, "What happens next?"

"That's a good question, but I think you already have the answer."

"Henry Bender, what do you mean?" Sara asked. The children had the same perplexing look as she did.

"Your future is now in your hands, and I hope you won't mess it up like my people did."

Roger asked, "How will we know what to do?"

"First, understand you are no longer restricted to this area. You are now free to live in the city and relate with the people."

Roger asked, "When can we start?"

"You can begin whenever you'd like. But I caution you to be patient, for all of this will be new to you. If you'd like, I will guide you." I realized that I would need all the help I could get for that to be accomplished. I continued, "There's much work to be done. We're going to see Father."

As Sara and I boarded a disk, Roger, as always, asked, "Could I go with you?"

Sara immediately said, "Yes, all of you can." The children formed a flotilla of disks and followed us into the city. Hopefully, they would also heed my warning to be patient.

Once in the city, they separated from us to land in the thoroughfares on their own initiative, which I thought was bold of them.

Father was pleased to see us and said, "Henry, despite the power being on, The Machine, other than performing the most basic tasks, is without direction. It will do little else until we give it specific orders. We do not know where to begin; it's been so long since we've had this much freedom we need help."

I followed my gut feelings and suggested, "Father, from what I understand from my day, I think there's a better way."

"Henry, if there's a better way, then we must do it. Tell us what must be done, for it's why you are here."

"Okay…" As I began to feel the pressure, I continued, "As I hope you are learning, the most crucial thing for people to do is to become self-reliant." Wow, it struck me, who was I to tell a smart thousand-year-old-man what was best? However, these people had spent their lives in inactivity, living without a purpose. With this great opportunity, this society now needed to create new aspirations to give their lives meaning.

However, they first had to deal with the basics. The food supply had to be maintained. Although the primary tasks were to control the operation of The Machine, which was not automatic any longer. It was now up to the people to make those decisions to initiate a path to survival. However, they needed a direction to follow, for it was their time to step up to the plate and perform. I could only help.

I thought of my world, where people made countless decisions daily, and could only wonder if these people would be capable of running things. Then a horrible thought struck me; if left alone, they might follow the same path they were on before. I had to make sure they were off to a solid start.

In the past, they readily relinquished their free-will in exchange for relief from their responsibilities. It was depressing to realize that this thinking led them to become entirely reliant on machines, which did start back in my day. If only people had taken the time to think things through instead of jumping on bandwagons of progress.

I said. "Father, ironically, being productive and accepting one's burdens with a purpose is what sets one free. It seems, at some point, that concept was lost. Have you ever heard the saying—*Idle hands are the devil's workshop?*" They looked at me with those blank expressions

Without any doubt, I continued, "According to the book of Revelation, it seems those who didn't go along with the trends and remained faithful were the ones taken out of harm's way. I understand how this all might sound bizarre to you. However, I believe it is the best explanation for what has happened to your world."

As we spoke, I was surprised to see energetic people crowding into Father's penthouse, who were now capable of looking into our eyes. Not knowing where they were coming from. I asked Father, "What's going on here?"

He said, "Henry, as you can see, things are changing—almost too much to process."

I ask, "Tell me what's going on."

"Henry, thanks to you, things are taking place we do not yet understand. Some who were treated have come back to life as if they were only asleep.

"Unfortunately, their knowledge only goes back to when The Machine first treated them. Nor do they have any memory of what took place while under those treatments. With a sense of urgency, he said, "However, we still have a machine and a city to run.

We need your fresh mind to make things happen. We are unsure what to do next, for we are a bit confused, and you must help. I know we will figure it out in time, but it must be expedited for us to survive. Your architectural skills are what is needed to restructure our society."

I felt all eyes in the room on me. If they only knew I couldn't manage my own life properly. Still, these people had messed-up worse than I ever could've. Maybe that leveled the playing field for me? So I stood tall and said, "Okay, let's get to work."

Father said, "Yes, let's get to work." The crowd cheered, inspiring us all.

Squeezing my hand, Sara whispered in my ear, "Yes, Henry Bender, let's do it." Wow! If people allowed life to be good, it could be great.

CHAPTER 38 The Plan

I realized this mission was not going to be about the work mankind creates to keep busy or make money. Instead, it's about the necessary work needed for survival. Taking charge of myself, I said to those who gathered to listen, "Our new social structure has to be a better concept than any of the ones tried before." Seeing the confusion in their eyes, I feared they might not be open to change, and said, "You must understand, if you repeat the mistakes of the past, you will be no better off."

"If there's a better way, tell us," Father again pleaded.

At that point, I wasn't sure what to say. Then, it occurred to me, and I asked, "Most of the old knowledge is still down in the Library, isn't it?"

"Yes, Henry, that is where it is."

"Father, mankind has lost its way. All that knowledge must be brought up from the library so all can reconnect with our lost roots. At the same time, we must develop a new and better plan."

Roger jumped in, "Yes, we need a new plan." I don't believe he knew what that meant, but when Sara squeezed my hand, I felt okay with it.

"Then we shall develop a new plan. All the books will be brought up. Henry, you will be in charge," Father decreed.

I was afraid he would say that, but I was eager for that opportunity. I knew it was not going to be easy, for it had to be an incorruptible plan.

Someone in the crowd asked, "What is the new plan?"

I had to improvise and said, "I'm just beginning to formulate it, and you must help me." Looking at their faces, it seemed these people simply needed a leader to give them a healthy dose of encouragement. At one time, most of them were smart enough to handle things, and I saw my task was simply to cheer them on.

I boldly said, "People were not made to be taken care of as if they were helpless domesticated creatures. You must learn to give as much as you take. This means you must learn to work and think for yourself. Tomorrow, we will start the work of finding one's purpose."

A cheer arose, and I felt a knot in my stomach, knowing if I failed, they would indeed run me out of town on a rail, so to speak.

As always, Sara felt my uncertainty and said to Father, "Tomorrow, we will start the work. But, for now, Henry Bender must rest."

Father agreed, and Sara and I flew to the Wilderness.

While walking along a path, she asked, "Henry Bender, what is troubling you?"

"It's just a lot of responsibility to take on. I don't know if I can do it."

"Of course you can. Henry Bender, you are the one who came to save us."

"Is that really true?" I added, "Look, I'm just an ordinary guy who screwed up and ended up here."

"No, Henry Bender, you are Special and will save us. I know this to be true."

How could I not love her? Impulsively, I challenged her to race me into the woods, although I knew she would beat me with her strength and my weakened condition. She led me deep into the woods, and it wasn't long before I was breathless. Seeing that, she stopped and sat on a boulder, waiting for me to catch up. I flopped down next to her, exhausted.

When I could breathe again, she looked into my eyes, and I knew, without her saying a word, what she wanted. We made love right there. Afterward, we laid in each other's arms for the longest time. It was as if we were the only two people in the whole universe. I wanted that moment to last forever, but knowing I had to deliver a new plan, I said, "There's work to be done. I must study up for tomorrow."

"Yes, Henry Bender, we must study up… What is study up?"

She delighted me, and I said, "I'll explain on the way home."

CHAPTER 39 A Time Of Discovery

All the books were brought up from the library. I was relieved when I didn't have to go along. At Father's place, I looked at the pile of what remained of all that people had recorded about the universe, whether it was factual or fictional. I was amazed at how little it seemed to be, without considering the high capacity of how much a thumb drive in this new world can store. Maybe a million times more than in my day.

Then, to my continued amazement, John electronically inserted all the books into one player, which meant it all fit in one's hand. Back in my day, some thought they knew all there was to know about life. Now, I could only think of how little was actually known.

Once back in our unit, Sara and I verbally browsed through the books. As I asked it questions, it brought up unrelated subjects, but the holograms changed to those giving the information I was looking for as I became more specific. It was an incredible research tool.

My background came into play as I thought about designing a solid foundation to build upon. Only, instead of it being constructed with steel, bricks, and mortar, as was my trade, it was to be built on our words and actions. Much in the way our founders started. Although I also understood the mechanical functions of the city were equally important.

I watched snippets from our history to help sort things out, going back to my day and beyond. I could see how the most critical issues were related to technological development. Which had taken precedents over our human behavior, diminishing our spiritual side. I could only wonder if this was done intentionally, and if so, by whom?

I hated to admit it, but I now understood how I was part of it by not actively participating. However, I was beginning to see how technological advancements might have caused some to believe they were superior to those who lived before them.

I lived in an age of dissension, where daily opposing protest sucked up one's ability to think for themselves. Where each faction thought they knew better and would say or do anything to win out. Allowing that type of thinking distracted them from working on the side where our human goodness dwells.

In effect, rather than making things better, it eventually led to a lopsided society. In denying our spiritual side, people sought status and material rewards for their behavior. Again, I had trouble understanding where these thoughts were coming from, for I never paid much attention to those issues. But, I've come to realize how important it was to have a purpose.

When I spoke to those who wanted to hear, I found myself repeating statements like, "I'm convinced we weren't meant to be less than animals led by a computerized machine. You must remember, as the story goes, *God created us in His image*, and we must live up to it. We're flesh and blood with a spiritual nature, engaged in the battle of *Good against Evil*."

Perhaps, I was going overboard in my thinking in the pursuit of what was best. However, it felt as if I was soaring on high; it was similar to the momentary highs I used to get while experiencing those foolish stunts of mine. I believed this newfound freedom would afford the opportunity to right some wrongs of the past.

I could only imagine what Phil would think if he saw me now. Oh, how I wished he were here. I said to Sara, "Since it appears the end of time had come and gone, it seems that those still here were condemned to live in an everlasting hell.

Still, as I remember it, the world was to end in the Apocalypse, which doesn't explain why these people were still here to live well beyond those times. I could easily be wrong in my understanding."

However, as I said that, I saw an expression of gloom on her face and found I couldn't just stand back and accept such a grotesque thought, for it was too depressing. I said, "I'm going to do my best to make sure things do not continue like this. I must help restore your people's lives, for human beings possess souls. It wouldn't be fair, for your only sin was to be born into the mess others caused. Sara, for your people to survive, they must learn about what took place."

Distressed in hearing what I was telling her, she embraced me, saying, "Henry Bender, you must rest now. You have a big day tomorrow; you will need your strength for the task ahead, and I also hope there is a God to help us."

I was pleased to hear her say that. I smiled and held her tight as we fell asleep in each other's arms.

In the morning, we went to see Father. His penthouse was crowded with energetic people. They flowed out into the streets, engulfing his building; the scene resembled some sort of vigil as if all were waiting for something significant to happen. As we entered, a silence came over the room, and Father said, "Henry, we have been waiting for you."

I'd never felt so significant, but I knew I couldn't let it go to my head, for I was still the same old guy, faults and all. They looked at me, waiting for a response. I took a deep breath and said, "I think we should backtrack to before The Machine took over. We need to know what led humanity to its lowest point, to when people gave up their natural rights." Again, seeing befuddled looks in their eyes, I realized they couldn't yet see how they had contributed to the decline of humanity. This called for a pragmatic approach.

I continued to speak, "I see the world through new eyes. First, as complicated as it might be, no one has the right to force their set of beliefs on others. However, there's a catch, we should never allow our innate *Evil* to prevail over the *Goodness* in us. To me, it's clear that *Evil* destroyed your world. You must understand The One's real purpose was to exemplify pure Evil.

"In my day, the problem was never in people having beliefs, or different opinions, for that's what gives us purpose. The problem was imposing one's narrow beliefs on all others, falsely assuming it was for the better good. Like saying, *do your own thing,* yet never seeing the deception in it. Not that I completely understand what it all is about. However, look where that simple saying has taken us.

"*Truth in love* is the only way *Good* conquers *Evil*. *Goodness* is only found on our spiritual side, for science cannot explain or control it. It is only able to numb us with treatments. People must come to their beliefs through honest and open discussion, which has become a lost art. Not to be drugged to solve the problems.

Many of the stories I was told as a youngster were designed to explain, perhaps the unexplainable." It felt good to share these thoughts. I sensed we were on the right track, heading to the right station where *Good* overcomes *Evil*. However, when I saw the perplexed look on Father's face, I realized it might be a station they weren't ready to get off at—or they even knew existed. However, I continued, "We must rebuild from the foundation on up. The first step is to strengthen those elements which give us sustenance. People must not expect a machine or any one person to dictate how one lives their lives. From now on, each must learn to take direct responsibility for what happens."

I felt a little odd. Was I making any sense? Then, out of the crowd, one asked, "How do we do that?"

Father said, "Let us not worry, Henry is here to show us."

There he goes again, putting it all on my shoulders. Yet I

knew in my heart, as crazy as it seemed, it was going to be my job to teach humanity how to live. I said, "Everyone must learn to think for themselves. You must never again allow a man or machine to do your thinking."

Further inspired, I continued, "We must never forget; at the base of all human behavior is *Good* and *Evil*. If you want to live in peace and freedom, people must live by a standard of conduct motivated by *Goodness*.

"It should be understood, we're not capable of thinking any better than those who came before us. The greatest power we have is to learn from past mistakes and make changes for the better. Not to rely on rehashing the past only to place blame.

"Since I've been here, the one thing I've learned was that technology is not capable of showing us how to think and act out of our natural *Goodness*; for that understanding comes from our spiritual side. Something you've disconnected from."

As I spoke, I watched Father; he was now smiling as if he knew this was supposed to happen. Oh, that's it! I now understood why these people kept calling me The Chosen One." It was not me. It was the message coming through me from that mysterious place that would set them free.

Knowing all could hear, I said, "It was not the Great War or The Machine that brought your downfall. It was allowing the *Evil* in us to take charge. When people gave their power away to technology, it allowed *Evil* to gain strength." As extraordinary as what I was saying was, I felt I was meant to speak of the revelations that now filled my head.

"What do you mean?" a voice called out.

My words came out faster than my mind could process them, but I allowed those thoughts to flow. "The Great War was caused by the *Evil One*, who, from the beginning, sought the power to control. The Machine knew no better. Ironically, when people gave their power away to technology, it took away one's will, neutralizing them." Shamefully, people blindly followed only to lose their purpose, reducing them to primitive survival.

"This brought on the end times, as predicted in the book of Revelation. I can only conclude, without proof of any kind or true comprehension, those who disappeared on that one day were actually the people of *Goodness*. God saved them from the devastation to take place, as He had promised. Yes, the *Evil One* and his most ardent follows were destroyed in the Great War, but those left behind didn't dispel the *Evil* still within them."

A meek voice asked, "Are you saying we are evil?"

"Well… Not exactly. I was referring to those truly evil people who were among those alive at that time; those who joined the *Evil* One." However, today, to choose good over Evil is in your hands." I felt to further accuse these people of what happened would not be fair.

"What are we to do?" another asked.

"Yes, that's a good question." I had to think fast. If something was to fill the gap in their thinking, it was to continue teaching the concept of *Goodness*.

I said, "For you to move forward, you must understand something critical."

"What is that?" a voice asked.

"You see, although The Machine was designed with good intentions, the most important point was missed. It was never capable of distinguishing the difference between *Good and Evil*, which allowed it to take your destiny away."

Another asked, "How can we find that purpose?"

You must reconnect with the teachings that will lead you there."

"How can we do that? Was it not The Machine's fault that we lost our way?"

"No, it was not. The chief sin was people's inability to understand The Machine lacked the human touch of compassion. In a distorted way, some people thought they could program love and compassion into it. But the transfer of that ability seems to be impossible.

"Consequently, The Machine decided the only way to deal with those who questioned its authority was to wipe out their purpose."

Father said, "Henry, I believe you are saying we caused our own problems?"

"Yes, Father, it does look that way. Only it wasn't any of you personally. Rather, the Evil in the world convinced many to give up their souls in exchange for convenience. *Evil* brought about the end times."

Someone pleaded, "What are we to do now?"

I said, "You must understand technology is neither *Good nor Evil*. It's only as good as what people make it to be. Science and technology have aided us in doing much good. However, at the same time, it's been involved in our worst atrocities that killed many. Even back in my day, too many bowed at the altar of technology, thinking it was the answer to life. In fact, in hindsight, dependence on only technology just about destroyed humankind.

"You see, The Machine's answer to bringing peace was to take away one's purpose, whether *Good nor Evil*, for it neutralized us. I know this was not the original intention of those who designed it. Yet, it was the result, for they failed to consider that such advanced technology could eventually develop a path of its own contrary to our human needs."

"However, let's not forget that a person's purpose isn't always good, for *Evil* dwells in the same space as *Goodness*. Since The Machine emptied your minds and perhaps stole your souls, it might now be wise to fill that empty space with *Goodness*. Consequently, I'm looking for the best system I understand works. It must be based on love and morality. Not necessarily in the way some present it. Many cannot help but corrupt what is good, which defeats us in the mire of confusion."

I wondered how it could be explained any better? But, I could only refer to what I knew and said, "Four thousand years ago a Special man taught about *Goodness*, and when he did, *Evil* couldn't stand it—he had to die. Through the ages, I'm ashamed of how his teaching has periodically been confronted with renewed attempts to kill his words. In the flesh, he had died, but his words live on. I can only think those who oppose the *Goodness* he taught continue to mount assaults to retain their unjustified power.

"Doesn't it fit the story of The Rapture and Armageddon? Yet, I'm at a loss to explain why humans were left to live on like empty hulks? Is that the way you want to continue living?"

Having said all that, I didn't know if the ground under me would open up and swallow me. Yet, I was without fear. I'd never felt this free before. It's funny how having a purpose allows freedom. Along the way, humanity had somehow forgotten all this. It was time to help them remember. They needed to see, first-hand, how people had come to this point. It was time to share the history books. In a sense, I was putting all my eggs in this one basket, hoping there were no holes in it.

I knew that they had to hear it from the primary sources to understand what I was saying. Fortunately, their books were easy to watch and listen to. In conclusion, I said, "To boil it down, you'll have to work your way through all the steps that must be taken. This includes your full involvement in the studies that will start tomorrow." I felt they needed time to absorb what I had said. Although, I still must admit some of this was even tricky for me.

I could feel the tension not only from the crowd but within myself. To lighten the mood, I changed the subject and asked Father how things were going on the technical side. He smiled and said they were still trying to work out the reprogramming of The Machine so they would retain the control.

Father went on to explain how much they had accomplished. With all The Machine's added circuitry stripped away, he said it was time to move ahead.

Finally, Sara said, "Henry Bender needs to rest." I was glad she did, for I never had to use my mind so much in one day. It was exhausting. However, to see Father smiling, as if he understood what all this was about, gave me hope.

Leaving them to continue their work, Sara and I bid our farewells and headed to the Wilderness.

CHAPTER 40 Discussing Responsibility

That night in bed, I wondered what these people thought of Sara and me being so close. Did they have any comprehension of what we were doing together? It's a tragedy most no longer desired to experience intercourse. Why was Sara more than able and willing? Was she the only one on this island who still was capable? With her in my arms, I couldn't think of anything else, and we made love again.

Afterward, I wondered, was she capable of carrying a child in her womb. Were any women capable? And now, with The Machine denuded, would people revert to the natural way of creating a family? I hoped there was enough information stored in the books to show these people how important and satisfying it would be. People were living longer; however, if humanity reached the point of not reproducing, wouldn't we become extinct?

This brought up another question; was The Machine still able to extend our lives? Fatigued from pondering all these issues, I closed my eyes and quickly drifted off to sleep.

The next day at Father's place, he reported, "Some are asking about work, for they do not understand the need.
"I said, "In a way, I can understand those feelings. From what I've seen so far, Father, I believe their inactivity caused them to disengage from the world and one another. They need to have interests, goals, and, most of all, a mutual purpose. Being kept like domesticated creatures, submissive, sheltered, and fed for no useful purpose was depraved."

"Henry, as you know, The Machine did everything for us, without asking for anything in return. They only ask, and perhaps with good cause, why must things change?"

"Father, is that what you think? Isn't it obvious? The Machine took everything from them in exchange for its so-called services?"

"Ah... Yes, Henry, of course, I agree. But not allowing The Machine to serve us at all seems to be moving backward."

"Father, sometimes going backward is not a bad thing. For the decision to exchange one's soul for the privilege of not working was not wise, and that's what was done."

"Henry, I do understand. However, most of our people have never known anything else. They are afraid of change."

I found his resistance odd. But I guess it was the same as when I feared to step out and start a firm of my own. Then it occurred to me; he was not trying to convince me of anything; he was asking for guidance. Even Father's thinking was asleep for centuries. Hopefully, in time, he will become fully functional once again. However, my immediate challenge was to persuade these people to take an active role in their lives.

I said, "I think the survival of your people depends on them having control of their destiny. But it does not necessarily mean The Machine cannot help in making their burdens lighter."

"Yes, Henry, but you must show us how." I saw it would be up to me to answer the age-old question about the necessity of work? I wondered if a mere architect with many faults was ever given a challenge so great. Yet, this did fit into my lifelong desire to design the best community ever, and I believe this conversation with Father was a good starting point to do just that.

Thinking back to my day, with the difficulties society faced, I wondered if it would ever be possible to have real peace and freedom. People of differing ideologies have always enslaved and killed one another in the name of supremacy. I reasoned; to be successful in this quest, it would be necessary to work from one set of rules. Rules I could only imagine would come from the mandates dictated by *Goodness*.

I said, "As you know, I've chosen the path I wish to follow. We do not need ideologies that embody *Evil*. The world just about destroyed itself in the conflict of *Good against Evil*. We should all try our best to never allow our freedom or purpose to be taken away again."

"Henry, then, as you said, new rules must be created."

In truth, I had doubts about being smart enough to contribute to creating a new set of rules that worked better? Many types of rules were formulated in the past, but all eventually were corrupted, leaving us where we are today. I guess all I could do was try.

Many thoughts flooded my mind I'd never had given much time and attention to. I wondered if all this was my doing or was I being directed. It's an incredible thought I might never find the answer to, so all I could do was formulate a plan and see where it takes us. My hope was it would lead us to a more purposeful life. Unbelievably, a new world, was born, and I was privileged to participate in its creation.

I said to Father, "I'm afraid changing your people's minds might be like the deposing of a god. If the concept of following someone who gives mercy and love won't be accepted, whether real or not, all might be lost. I understood the technology The Machine contains was important. But it was not a god."

Father said, "You are in charge."

I committed myself to that job. The first thing was for all those working on the reprogramming to gather.

When together, I instructed the team to prioritize The Machine's functions and only allow the ones that serve us well. That spurred much discussion concerning their concepts of work and responsibility. As I listened, at first, I felt as if I was in an alien world I couldn't ever escape from.

However, once the basic understanding of *Good and Evil*

was accepted, we could move ahead. For it wasn't that these people were *Evil* or lacked their natural inborn sense of *Goodness*. They merely had lost the ability to think for themselves. I began the instruction by stating, "The Machine practiced authoritarian rule, which prevented you from having freedom. However, there might always be those characters who continue to impose their control over others.

"In my day, society had become permissive in teaching the concept of being non-critical, which allowed those who could convince people freedom meant *that one could do as they pleased*, only to manipulate and gain power. That concept caused conflicts due to the many different points of view. It was the beginnings of irresolvable differences, for those who promoted it most were the ones guilty of being super critical of those who disagreed with them. There appears to be no end to how fallible and misguided people allowed themselves to become."

Since the first priority was to get the necessary apparatus functioning for our immediate survival. I established teams and assigned them precise tasks to help accomplish goals. I knew it would take time, and I hoped we wouldn't run out of the basics before achieving it. I stated, "Fortunately, there's plenty of food in the fields. However, we need to maintain the planting and cultivation of those crops. Hopefully, The Machine would continue to do the hard labor, but you must never again lose control of the operation. Which means you must all learn how things work. More importantly, without the rule of law, that rewards *Goodness* and punishes *Evil*, all will be lost again."

Seeing their looks of befuddlement, I suggest a training system had to be established to teach one how to distinguish *Good from Evil, Right from Wrong, Wise from Foolish, and accept the responsibilities' heavy burden of freedom.* Your will and actions must be filled with those goals."

In the days following that intense meeting, we began to gather in large groups to watch and listen to all sorts of books.

These people were not ignorant. In fact, they were once smarter than I ever was. The entire world had been in a deep sleep, their cognitive powers had to be reignited. Fortunately, by using the player's ability to enlarge the holographic images and amplify the sound to fit any size audience, from one to thousands, we were able to expose everyone to the books at many sites set up around the city.

This was an ambitious attempt, hoping to bring everyone up to speed. Thankfully, a remarkable transformation began to take place. It was miraculous as their rusty minds, now lubricated with knowledge, began to crank and shift into gear.

As I watched and learned from what was in the books, I knew that they would soon outstrip me if they were allowed. However, the most challenging thing was to get them out into the fields and oversee the manufacturing operations. Thankfully, they were capable enough to reprogram The Machine to perform a majority of the hard labor. This gave the people control of the day-to-day decision-making.

Equally important was medical care. Fortunately, those who were once doctors, nurses, and pharmacists before The Machine treated them. Even if treated lifetimes ago, they became active in abstracting and disseminating the up-to-date knowledge The Machine contained. Beyond it all, I still believed the most essential element was to find purpose in their lives.

As the weeks passed, I was encouraged. Most were settling into new routines. At that point, I felt compelled the time had come for me to give more attention to the spiritual side of our lives. To me, it was the key to open the door to beyond our survival.

Meanwhile, Sara wanted to know more about family life and the intimacy of love in my day. She wanted to be intimate every day, and it was a task for me to keep up with her.

Although, I welcomed it and certainly wasn't complaining, for my strength was returning, and I was putting on weight.

Fortunately, competent people were emerging and slowly taking charge of the city's workings, which allowed me the luxury of pondering what spiritual elements were missing and needed to be added to our newly established society. My personal priority was to restore family life.

Yet, I wasn't sure if it was possible anymore. Unbelievably, they found three infants living inside The Machine at different stages of growth, not yet old enough to move around and feed themselves. Fortunately, they were immediately taken out and placed in the hands of trusted old ones. Those who had memories of how mothers and fathers once raised a child.

On top of everything else going on, I couldn't help be concerned about how sexual intercourse might affect Sara. Not yet knowing if she was able to conceive a child? I knew the time was long overdue to talk to Father about it.

I thought it best to speak to him alone, which confused and distressed Sara. I was beginning to see she had more depth and personality than I initially thought. I told her I wanted to talk to him concerning a man thing. Luckily, I was convincing enough, for she accepted it.

It would be my first one-on-one meeting with him, and it felt as if I were naked. As if I was going to see my old boss, as irrational as it might be. I was set to meet with him in the morning.

As I prepared, I couldn't help but realize how vital Sara had become to me. I didn't want to lose her. I needed Father to help me understand what physical limitations she might have in getting pregnant.

CHAPTER 41 Receiving The Best News

In the morning, I arrived in Father's place, a woman escorted me to a small side room where Father was waiting alone. It was almost too formal. Was he expecting something big from me? He welcomed me and asked how he could be of help. I said, "Well, it's about… Well, Sara and I have been wondering…"

He interrupted. "Henry, I'm old enough to have had a personal mother and father who were among the last married couples to give birth naturally. Therefore, I have some understanding of the relationships men and women once had. Although when I was born, lifetimes after The Great War, things evolved, and it became a rare occurrence for a man and woman to have a close relationship. Unfortunately, by the time I was old enough to participate, it had become just about extinct."

As I listened, I realized I was acting childish. I believe Father already perceived my thoughts and knew what I was seeking. I said, "I'm sorry, but speaking to others about such matters has always been difficult for me. Also, it's hard for me to accept what is going on here concerning intimate relationships."

"Henry, tell me what it was like in your times," he asked.

Again, I felt it was up to me to take the lead. On the other hand, I also felt as if I was being led. Considering the millenniums between our views, I explained how men and women related to one another in my day. I also went into what little I knew about childbirth. I could tell by his expression he was most interested, although limited in his understanding.

He said, "I see… I have never been told of those details, for it was not spoken of. Let me tell you what I do understand and a little more of what happened since your times." From his history study, he explained it apparently started when women began to openly deal with unwanted pregnancies by using procedures and medications, especially those that terminated their pregnancies.

I added, "Yes, my society had become highly sexualized in all of its facets, which inadvertently led to many unwanted pregnancies."

"Yes, Henry, but rather than successfully promoting self-control and contraception, people resorted to quick fixes, which the abuses over lifetimes alter one's biology.

"People were either unaware or blinded to any future consequences. It still took many lifetimes before it clearly showed the effects on one's ability to conceive. Added to that malady, it also diminished their sexual desires. As I understand it, during your time's people became increasingly promiscuous with less regard for relationships. This caused them to no longer believe pregnancy to be an enhancement, for it apparently interfered with the lifestyles of the day. That behavior became so widespread, terminations eventually exceeded births. It took centuries before those adverse effects became unmistakenly evident in one's physiology."

I was staggered. Further telling me that marriage and family life eventually was no longer practiced due to the difficulties of one's reproductive functions, marriage, and family life.

Even in my times, I remember warnings of what might happen because of our indulgences. In fact, Cecilia and I wanted no part of it. We had hoped to have a large family. Sadly, we never got that chance. I hope she was able to find love and birth a family. Oh, how I miss her.

He went on to explain, "Added to those self-induced abuses, the Great War took a major toll with injuries, disease, poisoning, hunger, extreme hopelessness and fear running rampant. In those times, it was so traumatic it left most women no longer able to conceive and men unable to perform. After the war, times remained hard, and, with the loss of resources, science became too weak to deal with those problems. People lost hope."

He told of how, due to so few children being born, the population significantly decreased. Also, by then, the waters had almost engulfed them. They believed their island was the only land left above water. The population was reduced to less than a half-million without enough territory to expand in. Consequently, instead of celebrating a birth, people frowned on it.

Those conditions were horrifying. Father and his people had been through so much, I wondered if he and the rest of this society could understand the importance of family life.

It was also hard to believe their city was the only place still above water. I couldn't imagine there weren't higher places in other parts of the world that could support life. But, it was not the time to discuss it. Curious, I asked, "Why couldn't The Machine cure those human conditions?"

He said, "About the time I was born, the building of The Machine was still in development. It took a long time before success was achieved. When I came of age and was educated sufficiently, I participated in that work well before it was put into full use.

"Nevertheless, beyond that period, it took longer yet, before anyone thought it was best to turn the whole process of childbirth over to The Machine. Up till then, only medical people took care of those procedures. However, doctors and nurses were scarce. Despite protests, that responsibility was transferred to The Machine. The few women who became pregnant found it too difficult to deal with childbirth pain and afterward struggled to relate to their children.

"Consequently, artificial insemination was developed to be administered by The Machine, which completely bypassed the act of human intercourse. By the way, I believe it was in your times when the procedure of creating "Test Tube Babies," as I believe it was called, was first initiated. You see, those actions were not invented by The Machine."

"So you've known it wasn't The Machine's fault all along?"

"Henry, people did not realize that it was a mistake to program it into The Machine as is now clearly seen in hindsight. In the long run, it caused more harm than good.

I said, "Since it was known it wasn't The Machine's fault, for it was only doing what it was programmed to do, why was nothing done to stop it?"

"Henry, for the longest time, we mistakenly believed disease was the cause and blamed ourselves for not being able to cure it. We paid a high price for our mistakes." He again asked me to remember this process took place over hundreds of years, and by then, they believed it was too late to do anything, for almost all the people had unwillingly succumbed to The Machine's control. "There were those who tried to stop what it was doing. However, if one was discovered taking action against it, they were rendered mindless, while some even lost their lives. As a result, our primary goal became to survive with the hope that we would be saved one day. And now, Henry, here you are."

Wow! Not entirely understanding what he said, I could only think of meekly asking if he thought it was too late for anything to be done concerning childbirth. Still wondering about Sara's ability to conceive. "Henry, we believe in each new generation, there are a few women who are born receptive and fertile; the only problem is there are no men left able to inseminate them naturally. We call those women The Special Mothers."

Then it struck me; he knew what Sara and I were doing. Why that old dog! I said, "You've known what we're doing together all along, haven't you?"

"Yes. That is why we encourage Sara and you to be together. Out of the few we know of, we believe she is our prime

Special Mother. We have protected her, hoping someday we would see the first natural-birth in hundreds of years.

How that news overwhelmed me. I couldn't help but say, "You have made me the happiest man. Does Sara know this?"

"It was not necessary to tell her. We knew, if she were truly a Special Mother, she would follow her feelings. All that was needed was for you, a fertile man to come."

"Oh, boy… I must go see her."

"Yes, go on your way."

I sped to the Wilderness, where she was waiting. I picked her up and spun around. Before she even knew the reason why we both shouted with joy. After I told her, we ran into the woods, hand in hand, until exhausted. Then… Well, we did what comes naturally.

CHAPTER 42 Back To Life

Sara and I spent that night, and the next day, in each other's arms. Since formal marriage no longer existed, we created our own custom. We made love all through the day, which constituted our honeymoon. I felt no guilt about our situation, for we committed ourselves to become one, which in my mind made our relationship and copulation whole and acceptable, even in God's eyes as I realized that element was still vital to me.

I began to focus on us, saying, "We can't bring up a family in a world like this. There's much to be done."

She asked in her eagerness, "Yes, Henry Bender. What is there to be done?"

"We must work to create a healthy and loving environment for our children. To build a world free of corrupted thinking." It was still a giant leap of faith that she could conceive. I wasn't yet convinced she would until it was confirmed. These times were so bleak, causing people to be blind to reality, how could Father be that certain it was still possible?

When we met with Father again, we found him, and the elders had made tremendous progress. Able to extract all the up-to-date information and research equipment from The Machine without destroying its ability to function under their control.

But, there was even better news. When The Machine was shut down, all treatments stopped. Consequently, one by one, people began to emerge from their zombie-like state. In fact, rather than being feeble, as was expected, they reverted to the condition they were in the day before their first treatment.

It was mind-boggling. However, the tragedy was how

they had misjudged the state of those who were treated. In all those hundreds of years since then, if they would've known it was something not to fear, they might've acted more aggressively in dealing with The Machine. Although, now to cry over spilled milk was not productive. Yet, how stupid they were. But that's not for me to say.

Miraculously, no matter how many years The Machine had controlled them, they quickly became aware, although somewhat dazed and confused about what had happened to them. In effect, each was reborn, much the same as I had been. Of course, they were now behind the times in their skills and knowledge, for The Machine's development had outstripped them. They had to reconcile those lost years, for many had been doctors, scientists, administrators, and the like. They needed time to reorient themselves and catch-up on their knowledge transforming the city into a beehive of activity.

Mechanics, artisans, technicians, merchants, farmers, and laborers—people of all sorts awoke and rose up. It was a fantastic sight to see. It reminded me of the old legends of when a curse was lifted, and the people awoke and were set free. Everything was falling into place, and I felt we were going to make it.

We were now moving from surviving to possibly thriving. Yet, I still worried. I knew we had to make sure what took place would never happen again. Even before they were drugged, most had lost a spiritual connection to the things and the others around them.

Determined to do my best to keep this new world from being consumed by *Evil's* corrosiveness, I decided it was time to teach these people how important it was to reestablish their spiritual side. The side that delineates us from all other living creatures. It felt as if I was on fire.

Sara listened and questioned each of my pronouncements about life as we spent the rest of the day alone. It was one of the most exhilarating days of my life. It ended all too soon, and it took a while for my adrenaline to dissipate enough to fall asleep in Sara's arms.

CHAPTER 43 The Greatest News

Sara and I took on the responsibility, along with others, to look after the children. This included their development, education, and integration into the greater society. After awakening, the adults who engaged in watching the holograms and grasped what was being said about their history became inspired and eager to jump in and help. Overall, we understood it would take a lot more work to convince all the people that technology was not their god. Instead, it was only a tool to be used, and it would be up to them to manage.

As the work progressed, it was gratifying to see people learning how to enjoy life. This included Sara and me, for we couldn't help but enjoy life. However, one day, she felt sick. Concerned, I took her to the oldest human doctors for an examination.

To our overwhelming joy and relief, they told us we were pregnant. It had been hundreds of years since a man and woman had conceived naturally. I couldn't help but share the news with everyone about how fortunate we were.

As a young architect, I'd dreamed of building a community modeled on family life; yet, in my previous life, I'd just about given up on it. Now I had the opportunity to not only build a community but a whole city, perhaps even an entire world. I'd been given a second chance at life. What an unbelievable miracle!

Meanwhile, among those who came back to life and had the expertise to study why men and women stopped having intimate relationships felt confident since the awakening, there were now many women capable of becoming pregnant. And perhaps some men now also able to impregnate them through copulation. Only, they no longer knew how to initiate those kinds of relationships.

The old romance novels might provide some information to help them develop it, despite some of those stories being unsavory. Another resource was the ancient medical books, which showed how best to safely go through a pregnancy and carry out natural childbirth.

They carefully observed and studied Sara, for they could only guess what broke that barrier that enabled her to be a Special Mother. However, I was overjoyed with her, and we hoped it would eventually happen for all. So we embarked on teaching the notion of intimate love. It was fascinating to see how people had little trouble embracing the idea of it. However, it was much tougher for them to carry it out, for they had become unbelievably timid in those situations. They even had a fear of the mere act of touching, for it gave them such intense sensations. Which they were taught was not healthy. Not knowing, until we told them, it was the most beneficial thing they could do. Yet I felt confident that, in time, those connections would be restored, for it's our natural behavior.

With such undertakings going on, all I wanted to do was to be with Sara and our unborn child in her womb. For the time being, we withdrew to the Wilderness, knowing the people were now alive and capable of learning to take care of themselves.

Before doing anything more, we were given an additional blessing—the incredible gift of having conceived twins. Life is good.

CHAPTER 44 The Fulfillment

As our children grew inside Sara, we settled into a routine. Still, there was an enormous amount of work to do, for the city required a purposeful order and a spiritual harmony.

I said to all who would listen, "We can never again give in to our base human traits, which are to satisfy self, to gain power, to have possessions, and exercise the free-will to do as one pleases in place of practicing our inherent *Goodness.*

"Each individual, as well as a whole society, needs something to look up to, instilling purpose. As discovered in hindsight, if we neglect that goal, we'll end up in the very same situation that would enslave us.

"One asked, "How can we make sure we keep moving forward?"

"Unfortunately, there will always be those who will discount our spiritual nature and hold technology, science, or even themselves, as their god."

Another asked, "What about The Machine's part in this?" As far as I can see, it seems science and technology, who created The Machine, only see us as being a pile of living cells. Although I will concede, with its help, many marvelous things were accomplished. However, without having a clear human purpose, what's the point? In our earthly lives, there will always be those who succumb to the dark side, reaping harm and destruction on others."

"Tell us what we must do," another pleaded.

"In Ohganiea, we are on the threshold of constructing a society based on *Goodness.* I know it's been tried before, but it has always fallen short due to corrupt people. This time, with the participation of all of us, I know we can do better.

"The Machine took away your purpose. Now, with it no longer in control, we have the opportunity to start over to make it work. We've created a clean slate; what an exciting challenge. I hope you are as eager as I am to get on with it. Are you with me?" A collective cheer erupted from the crowd.

Meanwhile, I was never comfortable living in our unit. It was no place to bring up children, so I asked for and received permission to design and build a stick-framed home by the lake in the Wilderness. Sara and I liked being close to nature. We had spent so much time together there; it seemed only natural to make it our home.

In this short time, I had become known as a teacher, philosopher, and builder. Amazed about what has happened to me, I remember where I came from and try not to tell anyone what to do. Instead, I encourage people to think for themselves and to follow the simple rules of good behavior.

Then one night in the Wilderness, Sara and I was sitting under the stars by our new home still under construction. Relaxed and reflecting, I said, "I hope we will make the right choices for our children."

"Henry Bender, of course, we will. Everything will be fine."

"I hope so. I certainly hope so." I put my arm around her and drew her close as we gazed up at the sky. Suddenly, I exclaimed, "Look! There's the North Star."

"What is the North Star?"

Pointing it out, I explained, "It's the stationary star in the North Sky, which shows the direction one is to travel in." As I watched her studying it with her sparkling eyes, I felt warm all over. All of a sudden—the glow of the star radiated out, lighting up the entire sky. It only lasted a second.

She asked, "What was that?"

I stood, grabbed her, and danced around in delight. When we stopped, I embraced and kissed her. Befuddled, she asked again, "What was it?"

"It was a sign giving us direction, the same as it did four thousand years ago." I could hardly believe what I saw. But miraculously in my heart, I knew it to be true with certainty, and everything was going to be just fine, for I felt His guidance had returned."

Overwhelmed, I swept her off her feet and carried her into our partially constructed house, where we made love. During which she looked into my eyes and asked, "Henry Bender, so this is what life is?"

"Dear Sara, yes, it is. And let's live it."

She could only say, "Yes, dear, let's.

THE END

www.ingramcontent.com/pod-product-compliance
Lightning Source LLC
Chambersburg PA
CBHW060424180626
46817CB00007B/2655